P9-CAL-576

A FRIGHTENED KID
ON THE RUN

A missing twelve-year-old who might have—probably had—witnessed a murder a few hours earlier.

A missing twelve-year-old whose stepfather had been getting calls he suspected came from the Ku Klux Klan.

A missing twelve-year-old whose mother had put herself into a position to get mixed up with bad trouble.

And now Mark Shigata was going to have to tell all of that to Al Quinn, a man he didn't consider to be any kind of cop at all, a man apparently almost totally untrained and probably a redneck besides. But all the same Shigata was going to have to let Quinn know a lot of things about his personal life, because whether he liked it or not, Quinn had primary jurisdiction in this case.

Anne Wingate

Death By Deception

HarperPaperbacks
A Division of HarperCollinsPublishers

For Liz, who helped

This is a work of fiction. The characters, incidents, and dialogues are products of the author's imagination and are not to be construed as real. Any resemblance to actual events or persons, living or dead, is entirely coincidental.

HarperPaperbacks   *A Division of* HarperCollins*Publishers*
10 East 53rd Street, New York, N.Y. 10022

Copyright © 1988 by Anne Wingate
All rights reserved. No part of this book may be used or reproduced in any manner whatsoever without written permission of the publisher, except in the case of brief quotations embodied in critical articles and reviews. For information address Walker and Company, 720 Fifth Avenue, New York, N.Y. 10019.

This book is published by arrangement with Walker and Company.

Cover photo by Herman Estevez

First HarperPaperbacks printing: February 1991

Printed in the United States of America

HarperPaperbacks and colophon are trademarks of HarperCollins*Publishers*

10 9 8 7 6 5 4 3 2 1

one

IT WAS DARK.

She walked in stockings, very softly.

Sam wasn't there. Sam wouldn't be there. So why was she being so quiet?

Sam might be there. . . .

She moved about the room, packing. Quietly. Efficiently. She always had been efficient.

She wouldn't get many clothes. Just a few. She had to hide out for a few days, but after that she could stay with Wendy as long as she needed to, just as long as she could come up with some money. And she had to do that anyway. She and Wendy were the same size, and she didn't *want* the clothes Sam had bought her. But underwear, she had to have that; she was squeamish about wearing somebody else's underwear, even Wendy's, even though she and Wendy had always been close.

The jewelry box. Don't forget the jewelry box. There wasn't much jewelry in it; Sam kept the good stuff in the safe. The good stuff had never really been hers at all. It was really Sam's and she just wore it. But it wasn't Sam who gave her the box.

She loved the box.

The lid was a butterfly, a beautiful cloisonné butterfly, red and yellow enamel inlaid in a glossy black background. The wings were stretched wide and it was rich and glowing.

Sam would break the box if he came back and it was still here.

And if he broke it he would find what she had hidden in it.

And he mustn't. He mustn't.

Sam would break her, if he came back and she was still here, because he had told her never to leave and she had left, left violently, left loudly, and Sam had tried to stop her and the police had come and got Sam.

But she had to leave. He'd found out—

The police wouldn't keep him long. Her sister had told her that. Her sister had been laughing. She didn't understand. She didn't understand at all.

There was a sound downstairs. Not Sam. Sam wouldn't be back yet. There wasn't time for him to be back yet.

Not Sam.

Someone was walking toward the stairs, but not very quietly, not quietly enough, because he was a big man.

Sam was a big man.

Under the bed?

The bed was a waterbed, sitting right on the floor, supported by a wooden platform. The salesman had said you couldn't put a waterbed in an upstairs bedroom. But they didn't know Sam. Floors didn't collapse in Sam's house.

Out the second-story window?

Into the walk-in closet?

The windows were open. The closed suitcase sat on the floor, and the jewelry box with the butterfly lid lay on the bed.

The white curtains billowed very slightly in the breeze.

"Melissa!"

She didn't recognize the whispered voice. It might not be Sam.

"Melissa? Where are you, girl?"

She was very still.

After a while the man left. She heard him going down the stairs.

She didn't hear the front door or the back door. But the air conditioning was loud and the doors far away. She wouldn't hear the door. She hadn't heard the door when he came in.

Melissa waited.

Finally she slipped out of her hiding place.

The windows were open. The closed suitcase sat on the floor, and the curtains billowed very slightly in the breeze.

The box with the butterfly lid was gone.

two

THE ONLY THINGS JAPANESE ABOUT MARK
Shigata were his last name and his face, and he wasn't too
sure about either of them. For all he knew, his last name
could have been considerably changed four generations
ago when his family had staggered, rubber-legged from
weeks of seasickness, off the ship in San Francisco. And
the broad Western grin sat so easily on his angular brown
face that when he was living in Denver about half the people he met thought he was some sort of Indian. It had been
the same in New Mexico, where he'd frequently been ad-
dressed in Spanish, a language he spoke almost as little as
he did Japanese.

But now he was living between Galveston and Houston,
in not nearly so nice a neighborhood as he normally would
have picked (because Wendy had left him a lot of bills to
pay off), and for a few people in the area his being Japanese had somehow become confused with their outrage
about Vietnamese-owned shrimp boats operating out of
Galveston Bay. It didn't matter that he hadn't the faintest

idea how one went about fishing for shrimp, or that he was fourth-generation American.

He'd been born in an internment camp while his father was in basic training getting ready to go fight World War II in Europe. His father, bitterly ashamed of the attack at Pearl Harbor, had come home at war's end fanatically determined to root out all that was Japanese in their home. The result was that Mark Shigata did not understand Japanese-ness; he had no idea what it was like to be Japanese, except for his face and his last name. But he did know what it was like to be treated as an alien; not even his father's aggressive American normality could shield him from that. So he was used to prejudice.

But it wasn't easy for Gail. And Gail had too much that wasn't easy for her—to begin with, her age. It is never easy to be twelve years old. Nor was it easy for a child to live with her adoptive father, knowing that her natural mother was out gallivanting around with the boyfriend of the moment. And a blue-eyed blonde adolescent living with a middle-aged Oriental man—well, that was a little hard to explain at times, and people didn't ask him to explain. They asked her.

On top of all that, there was her babysitter. On the evenings when he got stuck in Houston until ten or eleven, or when he was suddenly called out of town overnight or for the weekend, there had to be some place for her to go or somebody to come stay with her.

Mrs. Jamison next door made an acceptable substitute grandmother. But Gail was indignant at needing a babysitter. She thought she was too old for that.

Eight-thirty. She should have gone to Mrs. Jamison's tonight, but the Jamisons were out of town for a wedding.

Although he really needed to work much later, he had left for home; he didn't like Gail to be alone at night. There hadn't been any real incidents at the house, but that didn't say there wouldn't be. And there had been those telephone calls. He didn't know how they had gotten his telephone number, which was unlisted, but somehow they had.

They. Person or persons unknown, though he had his ideas. The telephone company had put a lockout on the phone, for all the good it did; the calls had been made from Seven-Elevens and similar stores all over Galveston County. And there'd been several different voices.

But an FBI agent doesn't leave his telephone off the hook no matter what kind of calls he's getting.

He slowed down on his own street, feeling edgy at the sight of a light-colored sedan parked under the street light in front of his house. Somebody was leaning against the back bumper, apparently waiting for him.

Something prickled at the back of his neck. He couldn't call it fear, but he didn't know what else to call it either.

He unfastened the strap on the holstered .38 at his hip as he parked his car on his own driveway. He kept his jacket open, his right arm poised easily at his side.

A bulky figure detached itself from the rear bumper of the waiting car, the ruddy face becoming almost invisible as the man strolled out from under the street light. "Mr. Shigata?"

"That's right." He felt a little reassured. A person who has come to kick your butt in doesn't call you mister.

"I'm Officer Quinn, Bayport Police Department. Have you—uh—got a minute?"

"I've been at my office all day," Shigata said tiredly. "Why couldn't you see me there?"

"What office is that, Mr. Shigata?"

"Say, what *is* this?" What kind of a policeman wouldn't know he was talking to an FBI agent?

"Shigata, you're going to make time for me here or downtown. Which is it going to be?" The *mister* was ostentatiously absent. But the bluster didn't ring true. When this man played good cop, bad cop, he ought to play the good cop.

But apparently he'd been watching too many 1940-style detective movies to know that, Shigata thought, or else he wasn't really a cop at all. But if he wasn't a cop then what was he doing here? And for that matter, if he was a cop what was he doing here? The situations he'd been encountering the last few months making him more wary than usual, Shigata said, "I'd really like to see some identification, please."

Reasonably amiably, the man produced badge and identification card for Shigata's inspection. "Albert Quinn," he said. "You can't blame me for going by Al."

"No," Shigata agreed, "I'd do the same. And now I'll show you my ID and we'll be even, right?"

Quinn didn't look like a cop, in wash-and-wear trousers, unpolished shoes, and an open-necked shirt without a tie. He looked like a farmer. His face was beefy and his posture almost as bad as his grammar, but his gaze was keen and watchful as Shigata reached in his pocket, quite slowly so as not to make any sudden startling movements. Quinn read the identification and looked back at Shigata. "Well, I'll be damned! I'd-a sure never guessed—"

"That they let us in the FBI?" Shigata interrupted.

"Yes, Mr. Quinn, I can even eat in the dining car on a train, or ride first class on a plane. World War Two's been over—"

"I ain't fighting no war with you, Shigata," Quinn said. "I got enough war behind me already. What I meant was—"

"It doesn't matter, I'm used to it," Shigata said. "What brings you here, Mr. Quinn?"

"Al."

"Al?"

"I mean, call me Al, other cops call me Al. I guess, come to think of it, most everybody calls me Al. And what brings me here"—he retreated to the trunk of his own car, to open a brown paper evidence bag and take a box out of it—"is this. You ever seen it before, Mr. Shigata?"

"Mark. My name is Mark. Yes, I've seen that or one like it. Why?"

"Want to tell me about it?"

"Not particularly."

"Well, Mr. Shigata, I've really got to ask you—"

"Al, your interrogation technique stinks. Never ask a person you're questioning anything he can answer by saying no."

"Well, hell, Shigata, we ain't got no detectives here. This is a fourteen-man department, at least it's supposed to be, but the chief got fired and seven others quit and so right now it's a—"

"Six-man department. Sheesh." Shigata was examining the box, noticing grains of black fingerprint powder clinging to it.

"And look, I used to work oilfield security and I just come on the police department six months ago and I never expected to be working no murders, at least not this soon, for cryin' out loud."

The box clattered back to the trunk, as Shigata straightened abruptly. "Man, this jewelry box is my wife's. My ex-wife. Are you telling me my wife—?"

"Well, the broad—uh—the—uh—lady that was murdered, she sure as hell wasn't no Jap."

"Neither w—is my wife. What did she look like, the body?"

"Oh. Well—huh—" Quinn consulted a pocket notebook. "White female. Maybe about thirty-five or so. Blonde."

"Wendy's a brunette, but of course I realize that's subject to change." Shigata felt himself breathing hard. "Go on."

"Blue eyes. That's about all I got."

"Height? Weight?"

"Didn't I say that? Sorry. You wouldn't believe how tired I am. Well, call it five-six, five-seven. Kinda slim. Say one-twenty, one-twenty-five."

"Definitely no shorter than five-six?"

"Well—"

"Could she have been five-two? Did you even *see* her, man?"

"Hell, no, she wasn't no five-two," Quinn said indignantly. "I guess I know the difference between five-two and five-six, and yes, I seen her."

"You're sure about that description?"

" 'Course I'm sure. You know who she was?"

"From that description, how could I?" Shigata asked reasonably. "I don't know many of Wendy's friends— we've been separated about six months—but I guess I'd better take a look. Let me go in the house and tell my daughter where I'll be. I ought to see if I can scare up a babysitter for her, though. How long will we be? How far away is the morgue?"

"Medical examiner's office is over by Mainland Hospital, kind of on the line between LaMarque and Texas City. Shouldn't take over twenty, thirty minutes."

"In that case I'll just run in and tell my daughter I'm going back out. What put you on me anyway?"

"There was an address book in the jewelry box. It said 'Mrs. Mark Shigata' inside the front cover. An address in Colorado, but inside the book under 'S' it had the name 'Mark' and this address. And that's why I didn't guess your job, Shigata, because murder victims aren't usually carrying around cops' phone numbers."

"Oh well. Yeah, Wendy has—had an address book. I mean she had it when she was living with me. Was there a crane on the front cover?"

Silence.

"Was there a picture on the front cover of a white bird with long legs?"

"Oh. Oh, yeah, I believe there was." A chuckle. "You said crane, I was thinking heavy equipment, not birds."

"Yeah. It's Wendy's, I guess. You sure that body wasn't—"

"Mister, I told you what the body looked like."

Shigata nodded. "All right. What else was in the box?"

"Stuff. Jewelry. I mean, what do you expect to find in a jewelry box?"

Shigata took a deep breath. "Where'd the body turn up?"

"Shigata—uh—Mark—" Shigata wondered why Quinn

was finding it so hard to say his name. "It was found at six-forty-five this evening in the back alley behind your garage. At least I guess it's your garage, it's in the yard behind this house."

"It's mine. I'm tearing it down." This conversation was taking about four times longer than it should. Shigata guessed he'd have to listen while Quinn came to the point.

"The killing was called in by—" Quinn consulted his notes again. "By a Gail Collins."

"What?"

"Gail Collins, the dispatcher said. Or something like that. She hung up without giving her phone number or address."

"You should have found her easily enough."

"Maybe so, but half the people that live in this neighborhood aren't home. Seems there's some kind of shindig at the school tonight—and none of the ones we did find at home say they know Gail Collins."

"You didn't go to my house?" Shigata asked incredulously.

"Mr. Shigata, there ain't nobody home at your house."

three

"**N**OW, YOU WANT TO TELL ME WHAT'S going on?" Quinn panted behind him, as they came to a halt in a pink and white bedroom at the far end of the hall.

Shigata glanced around; he'd almost forgotten the policeman was with him. "You're right—she's not here."

"She who for God's sake?" Quinn demanded.

"Gail Collins. Your complainant. My daughter." Quinn looked puzzled, and Shigata said, "All right, stepdaughter. But I adopted her six years ago, and when her mother moved out she left Gail with me."

"Collins? She's married, then? Didn't sound old enough."

"You talked to her? I thought you said—"

"On the phone, not face to face. She give me the address where the body was, and then hung up. But she sounded like a kid."

"She is. Seventh grade. We didn't change her last name because of school records—she was already in school when the adoption went through. She ought to be here, though. I talked to her on the phone about four-thirty, after she got home from school, and she didn't have permission to go anywhere. And she didn't even ask to. She's got a cold."

"Oh shit." Quinn's jaw tightened as he followed Shigata into the front room. "You think—?"

"I don't think it's a snatch." Shigata sat down on a brown velveteen sofa and reached for the telephone book. "That's the first thing I thought of when you told me there wasn't anybody here. But I don't now. You can see for yourself there's been no struggle. It looks to me like she left on her own, unless she went outside and they grabbed—but I don't think so. I don't think so. I think she was scared and I wasn't home, so she left and went to some place she felt safe. I've just got to find out—"

There wasn't any answer at the babysitter's house.

There wasn't any answer at her best friend's house.

There wasn't any answer—

"Oh, hell," Shigata said, abandoning the telephone. "You told me there was a shindig at the school. She probably—"

But by the time they got to the school it was dark. The shindig, whatever it had been, was over, and the last cars were departing. "She didn't go there anyway," Shigata said, more to himself than to Quinn. "She'd have told me. She always tells me when she's got something happening at school. I try to go to them."

More telephone calls. She wasn't at the Jamisons' house; they were home now and alarmed to hear she was missing. She wasn't at Karen's house; Karen had invited her to go to the Halloween carnival with her even though she'd already said she didn't want to go, and she had refused, explaining again that she felt bad. She wasn't at Kristi's house; Kristi was spending the night with Karen, and she confirmed that Gail had been feeling really bad that day, coughing and sneezing. She wasn't . . .

"There's nowhere else she goes. I can't think—"

Al Quinn took the telephone out of Shigata's hand and dialed. "Quinn," he said. "I'm back out here at the scene. You know that complainant we couldn't locate? Well, she's twelve years old and she's gone missing. I want a lookout—"

"I'll handle that," Shigata said, almost in a monotone. "I'm FBI, I—"

"Sorry, Shigata, but this is my jurisdiction, not yours. At least not yet."

"Quinn—" He was almost startled to hear the note of despair in his voice.

But Quinn was right. The FBI doesn't have jurisdiction until a child's been missing over twenty-four hours—even if it is a suspected kidnapping—unless a ransom note has been received, or there is strong reason to believe the child has been taken interstate, or there is some obvious factor making it apparent it is going to be a heavy case. And right now Gail Collins was not a suspected kidnapping at all. She was only a twelve-year-old missing from a little frame house eight miles north of Galveston Bay.

A missing twelve-year-old who might have—probably had—witnessed a murder a few hours earlier.

A missing twelve-year-old whose stepfather had been getting telephone calls he suspected came from the Ku Klux Klan.

A missing twelve-year-old whose mother had put herself in a position to get mixed up with bad trouble.

And now Mark Shigata was going to have to tell all of that to Al Quinn, a man he didn't consider to be any kind of a cop at all, a man apparently almost totally untrained and probably a redneck besides. But all the same he was going to have to let Quinn know a lot of things about his personal life, because whether he liked it or not, Quinn had primary jurisdiction in this case.

"They'll call back in a minute," Quinn said. "They got two calls coming in on the emergency line. Give me a description while we're waiting."

"Yeah," Shigata said. "Okay. I guess—four feet ten inches tall. Blonde hair, kind of—I don't know what you call that kind of a haircut. Just a little-girl haircut with bangs. She says—Oh yes, she says the bangs are feathered back. Blue eyes. I already told you that."

"No, you didn't."

"Then—No, I didn't, did I? I was just thinking about it. All right—real slim, almost thin. I guess maybe, I don't know, seventy pounds? I don't know what kids weigh. Just a minute." He headed down the hall, returning moments later. "No clothes missing that I can tell, unless maybe she had something stuffed in her gym bag; in that case it might have been dark blue jogging clothes. This morning she was wearing white pants with thin pastel stripes, blue and pink and green, and a pink sweater. And sneakers. Pink sneakers. I think she has her purse with her. A small shoulder bag, white with turquoise trim, that Ocean Pacific stuff the kids all want now. The sweater's short-sleeved—Grab that phone."

"For you," Quinn said.

"Shigata—Yeah, Jim, that's a policeman, yeah, local. I live in Bayport, remember? No, she didn't—Did she say—

Jim, she's missing, we can't find—No, that's not—Jim, will you pipe down a minute and let me tell you? She apparently saw somebody get killed. There was some woman murdered behind my house and Gail called it in and when I got here—About six-thirty she called, that right, Quinn?" Quinn nodded. "No, they don't know yet. No, he described her to me and I don't think it's Wendy, but I've got to go look at—would you please? If you can—" He was silent for a moment. "Not that I know of. I mean nobody's burned a cross on my front yard, but that doesn't—Jim, for God's sake, I don't *know*—Okay. Okay, yeah, his name is Quinn, Al Quinn—No, that's Q-U-I-N-N. Look—Okay. Okay. See you."

Hanging up, he half dropped the phone. "My boss. He'd just remembered he'd forgotten to give me a message to call Gail that came in after I spoke to her. He's going to try to get the Bureau to come in on this now, because there's the chance—"

"What's that you were saying about nobody's burned a cross?" Quinn was eyeing him steadily.

"Oh, the damn KKK doesn't like me. You know they've been making that big stink about the Vietnamese shrimp fishermen, and—"

"So? You ain't Vietnamese and you ain't no shrimp fisherman. What has that got to do with—"

"I had to question some of them, and they took it rather personally. Anyway, you know, all of us slant-eyes look alike." He turned to head into the kitchen, adding over his shoulder, "Surely you've noticed that."

"No, I can't say I've noticed that." Quinn, right behind him, snatched the coffeepot out of his hand and added,

"Go sit down, man. You want some coffee, I'll make you some coffee."

"You don't have to—"

"Who said I had to? Where do you keep the coffee?"

"On top of the refrigerator. And I can—"

"That's a dumb place to keep it."

"So I'm a dumb Jap. I've heard that often enough. What the hell, Quinn, you're supposed to be on the same side of the law I am and you dislike being around me so much you can't even manage to say my name, so why don't you just get the hell out of—"

Quinn slammed the can down on the counter. "Sit down and shut up before I slap the shit out of you!"

"Before you what?" Shigata swung around to stare at Quinn.

Quinn reached into his hip pocket and pulled out his billfold, pitching it open onto the counter in front of Shigata. "Look," he said, "that's *my* wife and them are *my* kids and I don't want to hear no more 'dumb Jap' or 'all us slant-eyes look alike' crap out of you again."

Shigata picked up the billfold. "Where's she from?" He noticed his voice had steadied some.

"Vietnam. And let me tell you, we know all we want to know and then some about the fuckin' KKK, especially since her brother just happens to *be* one of them shrimp fishermen you was talking about and I sponsored him to come over. And I had a boy named Mark and a hit-and-run driver got him about eight months ago. He was just a little older than your girl. And so I know something you don't seem to have figured out yet, Shigata, and that is, you can be just as good a cop as you want to be, you can be the best damn cop in the world, but when it's your own family hurt, you ain't no cop, you're a victim, and you think like a victim and you react like a victim. Man, you're hysterical, and I'm telling you, it ain't gonna do no good. We never found out who killed my boy. That's one reason I left security and went on the police department, in hopes maybe someday I'd get a chance to find out if it was a real hit-and-run or if it was some sorry bastard that don't like slant-eyes. Now, I hope we find your girl all safe and happy, and I'm going to do everything I can to see to it we do. But it ain't gonna help a bit for you to keep running around having hysterics. And you'll have to excuse me if I call you by your last name, but just for your information your first name ain't one that's real easy for me to say right now. And maybe I don't talk no textbook grammar, and maybe I ain't been to all the Bureau's fancy schools, but Shigata, I ain't stupid.''

"No, you're not.'' There was a long silence before Shigata quietly repeated, "No, you're not stupid. And you're right. I was wrong, and I'm sorry. I was doing what I was accusing you of doing. But I—oh, hell, you know how it is. You get it so many places that after a while you start seeing it when it's not there.''

"I know. I do it, too.'' Quinn plugged in the coffeepot and slammed a cabinet door shut.

"I guess—I guess you're hearing a lot of my father in me now.''

"What about your father?'' Quinn opened another cabinet. "Where the hell do you keep the cups?''

"My father hated being Japanese. He hated us being Japanese. Talk about feeling like a victim—'' Shigata got up again and put two cups on the counter.

"Sit down,'' Quinn told him. "Where's the milk?''

"In the fridge. All right, you're right. About feeling like a victim, I—it's just—not knowing where she is, I didn't know I could be so scared, I—" He took a deep breath. "You want a sandwich? I think there's some bologna, unless Gail finished it off when she got home from school. She—she always wants a sandwich after school, only for her a sandwich is usually three or four sandwiches. I get her that chicken bologna. I think it's a lot better for her than the other kind. She eats a lot. Your kids eat a lot?"

"All kids eat a lot, leastways all the kids I know of. My oldest girl, Janie, she's allergic to bread. That don't help much either. How you gonna tell a kid to go get a peanut butter sandwich if she can't eat bread? You want to get that phone?"

Shigata stepped into the living room and then called, "It's for you. Your office."

Quinn relayed the description and asked to have it broadcast to neighboring departments. Then he said, "Shigata, I know you don't want to leave the house. But we got to get that body identified. Especially now. Because there's always the chance whoever got her might have—"

"Gail. I know. Don't say it. Let me get my jacket. I hope Gail's got a jacket. What's it supposed to get down to tonight? The temperature I mean?"

"Fifty-six or something like that. Not too bad. But she's got a cold, hasn't she? You said—"

"Yeah, she's got a cold. I hope she's indoors, wherever she is. I hope—" He wiped the back of his hand across his eyes. "You got a jacket, Al?"

"It's in the car. And speaking of cars, we better take mine. It's got a radio in it."

*　　　*　　　*

If you don't eat lunch at school, you can save a dollar and a quarter a day. If you eat a great big breakfast and you eat a couple of sandwiches just as soon as you get home from school, it's not too bad to skip lunch. And you can save a lot of money that way, and maybe if you save enough money you can help pay the bills.

Daddy worried a lot about the bills. He tried to explain to her that everybody has to pay their bills, but if you're an FBI agent it's especially important not to get behind on them, because people trust you. And—

He always stopped there. But Gail knew what he was going to say and didn't say. It was Mom's fault there were so many bills. Mom and all those clothes she kept buying. Some of the clothes for Gail, but most of the clothes for her. She had pretty clothes, very pretty clothes, but Dad had kept saying, "Wendy, you've got to understand, I just can't afford for you to buy so much, especially not at Neiman-Marcus and Joske's. What's wrong with Sears?"

Mom said the clothes at Sears weren't nice enough, and Dad said, "If you'd stay out of those damn bars—"

Mom said they weren't bars, and Dad said, "Nightclubs, then. You don't need to be—"

And then they both noticed Gail listening, and Dad quit talking because he didn't like to yell in front of Gail, and Mom laughed. And the next day she went back to Neiman-Marcus and bought four more dresses, and she bought a pretty nightgown at Joske's. She did that because those were the stores Daddy had yelled about.

Gail said she guessed Dad would like the nightgown, anyway, because he used to like to buy Mom pretty nightgowns. But Mom laughed that tinkling phony laugh that always set Gail's teeth on edge, and said, "Oh, you needn't think I'm going to waste it on *him.*"

That made Gail's stomach feel bad. She remembered what it was like before Mom married Dad, even if Mom didn't.

Then, in April, six months ago, Mom moved out. They had a big fight about that, and even Dad didn't care if Gail heard. He told Mom she could go alley-catting if she wanted to and he didn't guess he could stop her, but he was damned if she was going to take Gail to live that kind of life. Mom laughed—she always laughed when Dad got mad—and said she didn't think he could stop her if she really wanted to take Gail, and then she said something Gail didn't understand about round-eyes and slant-eyes and Dad called her foulmouthed bitch, and she laughed again and said, "But I don't want to, sweetie-pie, I don't even want to." And then she went away. A man in a big car came to help her get her clothes.

She went away without telling Gail good-bye.

But things were quieter after she left. In the summer Gail went to Mrs. Jamison's house in the daytime, and that was fun because sometimes Mrs. Jamison made cookies and she had a collie in the yard, and she didn't have headaches every morning the way Mom did.

In the fall, Dad bought Gail's school clothes at Sears and Ward's and Penney's. He let her pick most of them out, and she got clothes like the other kids were wearing. That was a lot of fun. They were pretty clothes. She had to be in the seventh grade again, but this year she was making better grades, and her stomach finally quit hurting and she quit having to take that yucky-tasting medicine in the blue plastic bottle. She never even opened the last bottle Dad bought.

But now her stomach was hurting again, and she didn't have the blue bottle with her. She knew right where it was, on the third shelf down. She didn't know quite where she was, though. And wherever she was, she was a long way from the third shelf down in the pantry at home.

Even after paying the taxi she had some money left. She'd counted. Six dollars. Maybe that was enough to buy some medicine, but then she wouldn't have much money left to buy food. She'd had supper, and she wasn't hungry yet, but she'd have to eat breakfast tomorrow, and at least supper if not lunch, and after that . . .

She didn't know what she was going to do. There was no place to go. She had thought she could go to where Mom was, but this couldn't be right, this crummy house a block from the beach, even though the taxi man said, "Girlie, this is the address you give me. Now, you want to pay me and get out of the cab, or you want me to call the cops?"

She paid him and got out of the cab.

She'd gotten the address out of Dad's address book, where he wrote it down the time Mom called, asking for money.

But surely this wasn't where Mom was. And even if it was, she must not be home, because nobody would come to the door.

And she couldn't go home—she couldn't—not after—

She still couldn't quite believe what she'd seen. She'd called his office. He'd told her he was going to have to work late; that would be where he was, at work; it couldn't have been him . . .

But she called his office again and that friend of his named Jim said, "Sorry, baby, I haven't seen him since about two o'clock. I figured he'd be home by now."

It couldn't be—Daddy wouldn't—

She began to cry again.

A big black man stopped on the stairs and said, "You wants to come inside, baby?" He leaned over her. His eyes looked funny, and his hand was hot when he touched her.

But the lady with him put her hand on his arm and said, "Leave the baby alone. You don't need no baby when you gots me." She had long fingernails and she smelled nice, like flowers, but she laughed just like Mom did, that tinkling phony laugh.

The man let her go, and Gail got up and ran away. After a while she found herself on the beach. She got her jogging jacket out of her gym bag, but even with it on she was cold, because the wind was blowing across the bay. The air smelled wet.

Gail hoped it wasn't going to rain.

There were some boards all piled up near the granite-and-concrete breakwater. Dad had told her the breakwater was so that if there was a bad storm it wouldn't be able to wash out the whole beach. She sat with her back to the boards. There was a little hole behind the boards. She could get into it, but she didn't know if she wanted to or not. There might be a crab in it. She had found a crab in a hole once, and it bit her.

Well, pinched her. Daddy said crabs didn't have teeth.

A fat man with a lot of tattoos walked down the beach. He had on a sleeveless shirt, and he had a mustache, and his big wide belt jangled. She'd seen him a while ago on a motorcycle. He stopped. "You lost, kid?"

His voice sounded funny, and he leaned over her and his breath smelled funny, like Mom when she got home late at night. "Go away," Gail said breathlessly. She scooted behind some of the boards, almost into the little hole.

"Be like that," the man said, and shrugged, and walked on down the beach.

Sea gulls called.

The big lights like streetlights went out.

It was dark on the beach.

Gail was afraid to go to sleep.

She might see *that* again in her sleep.

If she crawled all the way into the little hole . . .

four

"I DON'T KNOW," SHIGATA SAID.

The lights were bright in the morgue off Texas Avenue. The woman lay on her back on a metal rack. Quinn's description had been accurate, as far as it went. She had fair hair, blue eyes; she was about five-seven, maybe a hundred and twenty pounds. Good figure. Long eyelashes. She'd been pretty once, Shigata guessed.

But he had to guess.

"What do you mean, you don't know?" Quinn sounded irritable.

"Just that. I don't know. She looks familiar, but I can't place—What the hell did he hit her with, anyway?" The right side of her face was crushed; the eyeball lay grotesquely down on the cheekbone, still tenuously attached by strands of tissue, and brain matter was oozing out of the eye socket.

"A chunk of old two-by-four with a couple of nails attached. It was laying in your back driveway, like he started to take it with him and changed his mind. No doubt that was what was used; there was hair and blood and brains on it."

"I told you I've been tearing down the old garage back there. That's probably where it came from."

"I guessed that. Which means it was spur of the moment. If he'd gone there to kill her he'd have taken something with him."

"Unless he meant to frame me. Which is not impossible. I'm beginning to have this feeling he's done a fair-to-moderate job of it whether he meant to or not."

"I hope," Quinn acquiesced gloomily, "that you can prove what time you left your office."

"I was in downtown Houston talking with the special agent in charge at seven-thirty. That good enough?"

"It is for me. It ought to be for the district attorney too."

"There's damn sure no way you're going to be able to print a picture of her in the paper and find out who knows her," Shigata commented. "Has she been fingerprinted?"

"Yeah, the Galveston ident people took care of that. But she's not in their files. We've sent a set of prints on to Houston. If they don't make her, we'll pass them on to Austin and then to Washington. But you ask me, I say she's local. Galveston or Houston, maybe Corpus. No farther than that. She's a beach bunny. Or a beach rabbit; anyway—maybe she's getting a little long in the tooth for a bunny. But anyhow, I'm guessing if she ain't in files somewheres in Texas then she won't be in files at all."

Shigata, who was inclined to agree, went on looking at the body. A vague thought was wandering through his mind that maybe Al Quinn was a better investigator than he took credit for being.

Designer jeans. A designer shirt. But the kind available

at hundreds, maybe thousands, of stores in the area; nothing that would be identifiable. And there wouldn't be any cleaners' marks because these clothes would have been washed at home or in the laundromat.

Sandals. Quite ordinary sandals, multicolored pastel leather. They hadn't come from K-Mart, but they hadn't come from Neiman-Marcus, either.

No jewelry.

No sign she'd been in the habit of wearing much jewelry. Certainly not a wedding ring, anyway.

And she'd been able to find plenty of time to lie in the sun. She had long golden legs and long golden arms, and her blonde hair may have been helped along, but it had been helped professionally. Very professionally. She'd had a nice smooth manicure, almost certainly professional, and a nice smooth pedicure she'd have had to be a contortionist to give to herself that neatly.

Pierced ears, but no earrings.

No callouses on her hands. Smooth hands, no reddening or thickening. That didn't say much though. Lots of jobs don't mark the hands, and most women have dishwashers now. But there was something about her—even brutally dead, there was something about her.

"She was expensive," Shigata muttered half to himself.

"Call girl, maybe?"

"Maybe. And maybe not. You can't say for sure. At least I can't. Just—she was expensive. Al, I think I've met her. I can't put a name to her and I don't think I met her on business. At least not on my business." Quinn chuckled involuntarily, and Shigata glanced at him and grinned ruefully. "And I don't feel deprived enough yet to start buying it. No, I think I met her socially, and I can't think where. But I tie a voice to her. A little light husky Marilyn Monroe-type voice. Before my wife left, she liked to party a lot. Nightclubs—she liked to go to nightclubs. I just couldn't go every night, not and get up and go to work in the morning, but I went with her some on the weekends. Seems like I met this girl at a nightclub. I don't think I met her more than once. I think Wendy told her my job and she got—silly. You know."

"Expensive," Quinn repeated thoughtfully. "Nothing else?"

"I'm sorry. If I remember anything else I'll tell you. How'd she get in my back yard, anyway? You got her car located?"

"How are we going to locate her car when we don't know what she was driving? There wasn't anything in a one-block radius of your house that didn't belong there. That's as far as we got. What I'd like to know is how your wife's jewelry box got beside the body."

"Yeah," Shigata said, feeling fairly sure he knew what Quinn was thinking, but not wanting to be the one to put it into words. "You know, that box might not be my wife's anyway. It's not unique. I think I bought it at Zale's in Denver. One of those big chain jewelry stores anyway—I'm pretty sure it was Zale's. I gave it to her before we were married. I'll admit the address book sounds conclusive, but I'd still like to have a look at the other stuff in it." He glanced again at the body. "Wendy's that type, too. Expensive. Too expensive for me, only I found it out too late."

"That hurts."

"Yeah. I should have had better sense than to marry her. But she was pretty. And she was fun, when she wanted to be. Then, too, there was the kid. I was sorry for the kid."

"You love her? Wendy, I mean?" The body was being wheeled back into the cold room.

"I thought I did. No, I guess I didn't. I could have. If she'd made any effort. But she expected me to do all the caring and all the giving in, and after a while I got tired of it."

"I hear you. Let's head on over to my office."

"I thought you said you weren't a detective," Shigata said fifteen minutes later, sitting in what was quite clearly a very small-town detective bureau.

"We had all those people quit at once," Quinn reminded him. "They had to stick somebody in here. I'm the somebody. Well"—he was digging through his desk drawer—"this is what was in the box."

"Okay, yeah, that's Wendy's address book. But I guess we already knew that."

"You want to—" Shigata looked up, half smiling, and Quinn flushed. "I want you to leaf through it and see if there's any names that weren't in it when she left."

"I'm not sure I'd know that. I gave the book to her the first Christmas we were married, but I never used it myself. I went on keeping my own address book. About all I can do is tell you the names I don't recognize."

Ten minutes later he said, "Al, there aren't ten names in there I *do* recognize."

He didn't need to add that almost all the names were men's. Quinn would have noticed that for himself.

"What about this?" Quinn dumped a pile of costume jewelry out of a plastic evidence bag onto the desk. "You recognize any of this stuff?"

"Uh-uh. Well, maybe these earrings. I don't know. Wendy had a pair like them. But I got them down on the Strand, in Galveston, and I shouldn't think they'd be unique. Other than that—but Wendy's been gone six months. Al . . . You know what we haven't done?"

"What's that?"

"At least I haven't. Called Wendy. I don't *think* Gail would have gone there, but—"

"But it's not impossible. No, I haven't called her, and I've got to talk to her, whether Gail is there or not. But hell, until I met with you I kind of figured that corpse *was* Wendy Shigata. You got her phone number?"

Shigata had a memo book in his coat pocket, with a few phone numbers scrawled in it. He leafed through it. "Yeah. Here it is. Phone number and address both. It's just off the East Beach. I drove out there one time out of curiosity, to see what the place looked like. Scoot that phone this way."

But the phone buzzed fruitlessly in his ear, and he hung it back up and shook his head.

"Shigata," Quinn said, " we could send the Galveston police over there to look for her, but I think—"

"Yeah. Me, too. But give me a minute to call my house first, just in case Gail's decided to go home."

Halfway to Galveston, Quinn said, "Shigata?"

"Yeah?"

"You know I might wind up having to arrest your wife for murder."

"I know."

"You think she could have done it?"

"I don't know any reason why not," Shigata said. "She

plays a lot of tennis. She runs. She's strong enough. And she doesn't have any moral scruples to get in her way. But I don't know of any reason why she would have done it, either.''

"Shigata, is your wife a call girl?" Quinn made his tone impersonal. That is not a question a man likes to ask another man.

There was a long silence. Finally Shigata said, in an equally impersonal tone, "I think so. At least she's not hurting for money, except for one time when she bummed a couple of hundred from me, and she was sick then—I told her I wouldn't have given it to her if she wasn't. And so far as I know she doesn't have any kind of normal job.''

"You know who's running her?"

"No. But I'm pretty sure somebody is. She's no businesswoman, Wendy's not."

"She asked you for a divorce?"

"Uh-uh."

"You asked her for a divorce?"

"Uh-uh."

"Why not?"

"Gail. I'm afraid she'd get custody. She doesn't want her, she doesn't love her, I don't think she even *likes* her, but she'd do it out of spite. And she'd get it, if she tried. There's no doubt of that."

"Well—"

"Don't kid yourself, Al. Adoptive father, different race? I'd get custody, maybe, if she was in prison and we got the right judge. But the wrong judge, he'd take her away anyhow and stick her in a foster home. Any other way, they wouldn't even talk to me. And you know it."

"Okay. You're right. Yeah, she'd get custody, damn it.

So what happens if your wife is arrested for murder? Don't they call that embarrassing the Bureau?"

"I expect that would embarrass the Bureau, yes. But no, they wouldn't fire me. I'm forty-three, and I've got nineteen years of service. They might retire me early, or they might call me into the home office to sit it out until retirement, or they might exile me to South Dakota, which wouldn't be much of an exile because I happen to *like* South Dakota. But I don't think they'd fire me."

"Too bad," Quinn said, half grinning. "My department sure does need a good chief." The car jerked to a stop before a small frame house that shared a concrete staircase with three other small houses. White paint was peeling off, exposing weathered wood siding. "That's some more kind of a dump."

"Your department wouldn't want me. And that place might not have been too bad before the last hurricane."

"It might not have been too bad before the storm of nineteen hundred. We ought to have a Galveston unit with us. Professional courtesy."

"I have to take a Galveston cop with me to visit my wife?"

"She ain't my wife. Thank God."

"You want to call for one?"

"No," Quinn said.

It didn't matter. Nobody came to the door.

Shigata took a credit card out of his billfold and looked at it, speculatively. He looked at the door and back at the car. "This is illegal, you know," he told Quinn.

"Yeah, I know."

"You want to wait in the car?"

"You sure you know how to do that?"

"I've seen it done, but I never did it myself."

"Then gimme the card. . . . Hell, man, the door ain't even locked—Oh shit."

Galveston, in October, is usually hot in the daytime. But even so, that smell hadn't built up in one day; it had been, at a guess, two days, maybe three. "Where?" Quinn asked.

"I've never been inside. This way, maybe?" Shigata used his pen to hook the bathroom door open, and then involuntarily gagged.

"Oh shit," Quinn said, gagging also. "I smelled that in Nam, and I wasn't planning on—Oh shit. Oh shit. Is that—?"

"Yeah. Which one of us stays here, and which goes to call the cops?"

"We're cops."

"With no jurisdiction here."

"Look, it's your wife, you go call the cops. I'll wait here."

"If it's my wife it'd be a lot easier to me to explain what I'm doing here than it would be for you."

"What do you mean *if* it's your wife, is it—?"

"Hell, yes, it's Wendy. I—Yes, it's Wendy." He swallowed hard. You had to know Wendy well, to know this was Wendy now.

"Then I want to be able to swear I didn't leave you alone here," Quinn said.

Shigata stared at him. "Oh my God," he said slowly. "Oh my God. I didn't think of—"

"I know you didn't think of that. But you'd better. You've got a motive. She was embarrassing the hell out of you and the Bureau. She was screwing other men and you weren't getting any. She was asking you for money."

"Once."

"But I'll bet you sent her a check, not cash."

"Well, yeah—"

"So you can't prove she didn't ask again. And you wanted shut of her in a way that would let you keep the kid. I'll bet everybody who knows you knows that. It's going to be hard to prove an alibi, because it's going to be next door to impossible to establish a time of death. I don't want to drive another nail in your coffin, man. I wish we could just say let's get out of here and let somebody else discover the body, but there's too much chance somebody saw us come in. Here's the car keys. Tach three is city-to-city—that'll get you Galveston dispatch. Go call the cops. I'll wait here."

five

WENDY SHIGATA MIGHT HAVE LOOKED EXpensive on Tuesday afternoon. But at eleven-thirty on Friday night, all she looked was dead.

Very damn dead.

Somebody might have meant it to seem accidental. She was naked, lying in a bathtub full of water. Jeans, shirt, panties, bra were draped across the closed lid of the laundry hamper; a blue satin robe hung from a hook. Her dark brown hair trailed in wet rats along her shoulders; most of her makeup was off her face and smeared on a white wash cloth.

Mark Shigata could have told them that was wrong. She always took her makeup off with cold cream.

But nobody asked him. Nobody wanted to talk to him at all. A patrolman had told him he had a right to remain silent and so forth, and he'd said he knew that. The patrolman—a rookie, at a guess—said, "Then do it, please. I'd rather you just wait and talk with the detectives."

So far the detectives hadn't wanted to talk with him.

They'd let Quinn explain how they happened to find the body. They hadn't asked anything else yet.

But anybody could see that any intended semblance of accident was utterly spoiled by the dark blue hand marks on her neck that told of a crushed hyoid, definitive proof of mechanical strangulation, and the unnatural position of her head had suggested she probably had a broken neck as well.

Besides all that, blood had splashed from the massive wound on the right side of her head—the side that was now leaning against the bathroom wall—all over the bedroom.

Shigata wondered whether they'd intended to burn the house. Either that, or they'd hoped it would be a very long time before the body was found. But even a lot of time wouldn't erase the evidence of bloodshed in the bedroom. No, they must have planned to burn the house, and hoped the police would find her dead in the bathtub and think she'd been drunk and not noticed the fire when she went to bathe, and not check any further.

He wondered why they hadn't gotten back to burn the house.

If that had been the plan.

Whoever they were.

Then he wondered, why he had thought of burning at all. He'd never, himself, seen an arson. And you don't normally think of burning a body in a bathtub. So there must be some reason—slowly, laboriously, he traced the thought back to its origin. A smell of gas. A smell of gas almost, but not quite, masked by the smell of death—but to get through that smell of death it had to be a lot of gas.

Somebody had turned the gas on somewhere in the

house and left it on. Left it on for days. For however many days it had been since Wendy died.

Wendy?

Not likely.

"Quinn?" he asked.

"Yeah?"

"Did somebody turn the gas off?"

"Yeah, it's off."

Quinn didn't ask how he knew it was on. But somebody else would ask. Or would not ask, which would be even worse.

Because the house was much too full. Captain Roy Hidalgo had arrived from CID, bringing with him Detective-Sergeant Lonnie Massey. Sergeant Donna Gentry had arrived from Ident, driving a Bronco full of lab gear and accompanied by Investigator Phil Conroe, also from Ident. Captain Matthew Dean from Ident was supposed to be on his way. Which made sense. In most places Ident works crime scenes.

Patrol division was represented by Sergeant Raoul Garcia, Officer Judith Chan, and Officer Willie Brown. Investigator Joel Morgan from the medical examiner's office was morosely taking his own set of photographs.

And Mark Shigata and Al Quinn were standing in the middle of the living room, ignored.

It added up to eleven people when Dean arrived, which he did while Shigata was counting. Shigata knew Dean; he also knew Hidalgo, Massey, and Gentry.

Eleven people alive, and one dead, in a small house that smelled like a three-days' battlefield. Plus the emergency medical technicians waiting outside to transport the body.

Shigata wished a lot of the people would go away, but

none of them showed any sign of doing it. And most of them acted as if they had forgotten they knew him.

Captain Matthew Dean did at least say, "Sorry, Mark," before he politely asked to see Shigata's hands. Emotionlessly, he told Conroe to photograph Shigata's hands. He very politely said thank you—whether to Conroe or Shigata was unclear—and disappeared back into the bedroom, asking something about a broken lamp.

Shigata wished all the people would go away. He wished—

Wendy had moved out six months ago. He couldn't remember now how long before that it had been when he realized he didn't love her and probably never had.

But he'd been married to her five years. He'd known her for nearly six years. She'd been wonderfully, vibrantly alive, and he'd appreciated that about her even when he'd begun to resent the fact that the liveliness was no longer aimed at him.

There were bright lights. People were still taking pictures, in the bathroom and the bedroom and the living room.

There was a lot of loud noise. People were talking.

People were laughing.

They shouldn't be laughing.

But to them it was only a crime scene. None of them had held that body, now dripping with body fluids, swollen and bloated with the gases of decomposition—none of them had kissed that face—

He was sick, so suddenly and unexpectedly he didn't even have time to lean over or turn his head.

There was a roaring noise in his head and the lights were dim and far away.

FBI agents don't faint—cops don't faint—I can't—

"Keep your head down, man. No, don't fight me, just try to relax—no, you've got to keep your head down."

"Al? Al, I—"

"Tell me later. Get you a deep breath. Come on, another one."

He vomited again. And again.

There wasn't anything left in his stomach to vomit, but his body didn't know that. He kept retching, and when he tried to lift his head all the lights swirled and dazzled—

"Get those EMT's in here. I think he's having a heart attack."

He didn't need an EMT. His chest didn't hurt. He'd be okay in a minute, when he could stop vomiting.

Somebody put a belt around his arm. A belt or something like a belt. Somebody asked, "Are you okay?" and then said something about blood pressure.

"Uh-huh," he said. He'd stopped retching. He wondered when that had happened.

Somebody said something about shock. "Uh-huh," he said, " 'm okay. Wait a—"

Somebody was taking his shoes off.

That was ridiculous. He could take his own shoes off.

Somebody was taking his jacket off. Somebody was unbuttoning his shirt. He tried to protest.

His arm hurt and he yelped. Yelped like a whipped dog, because he didn't know why—

"Just a shot. You'll feel better—"

"Had all he could take and then some." That was Al Quinn's voice, loud and angry. Al didn't need to be angry. It wasn't their fault. Galveston has a good police department.

Shigata would tell him so. In just a minute. When the swirling mists got out of his head and stomach.

Somebody asked, quickly and loudly, "Did you kill her?"

Somebody shouted, "Al Quinn, you son of a bitch, what do you think you're—"

"No," he said. "No!" he shouted. "No, I didn't— Where's Gail, where's Gail, where's Gail—please— Gail—please—find—"

The shot hit him then.

She sat on the curb of the seawall, facing away from the ocean, huddled inside her almost useless jacket, watching the lights come and go. She'd lost count of the police cars. There'd been two ambulances. That big car like a cross between a van and a station wagon—a blue and white car like a police car but not exactly—people and people and people, and lots of bright lights.

There hadn't been sirens.

But one of the two stretchers they'd brought out had been covered all the way. That meant somebody was dead.

That meant somebody was dead in that crummy little house where the cab driver had made her get out.

Maybe her mom was dead.

She ought to care. But she didn't guess she did care very much.

She wanted to go home. She wanted to go home where her dad was, only her dad wasn't there because she saw him go inside the little house, him and another man, and then her dad came out alone and got in the car a few minutes and then went back in the house, and she didn't see him leave a second time. But she wanted to be at home.

She wanted to go eat supper and take a bath and get in her own bed. She wanted some medicine out of the blue bottle, and she wanted a glass of milk.

And she wanted to go to sleep.

Somebody was walking along the beach. She couldn't see the person, but she could hear him. He walked like he was heavy.

He went past her and up the stairs and down the sidewalk.

Somebody was driving on the beach, driving wild, driving crazy, driving in circles.

There was a ramp going back down to the beach, but she was scared to go there until that car went away.

A siren. The beach patrol. Daddy had told her the beach patrol was the sheriff's department, not the city police department. She sat curled on the seawall, sitting small, merging with the shadows, watching.

The deputies shouted. The men who had been driving in circles shouted. The deputies put handcuffs on them and searched them. There was something in their pockets, and one of the deputies told the other deputy he ought to have known.

Gail sat and watched.

Another beach patrol came and joined the first. Then one of the beach patrol cars drove away with the men who had been driving in circles. A while later a wrecker came and took their car away, and the second beach patrol left.

Gail slipped back into her hidey-hole behind the boards.

She was cold, and she had begun coughing again, but she was so tired she went to sleep anyway.

*　　*　　*

Melissa felt as if she had been running forever, all to get back to where she had started from. Back to Sam's house, and she didn't want to be at Sam's house.

But Sam wasn't there. She didn't know where Sam was. She'd seen him on the beach, but he hadn't seen her. That was a couple of hours ago, and she was hoping she could be through here and gone again before he got back.

Hoping.

She had to, that was all. She had to have more clothes, because she wouldn't be able to borrow clothes from Wendy, after all. She nearly started to cry again at that thought, but she didn't, because if Sam came back he would hear her if she was crying.

Besides, she had to work fast.

Work fast and get away.

If she just knew where Gail could be—

Her throat hurt more than ever, with that thought.

None of it made sense. Wendy went away and left Gail? She wouldn't, she wouldn't, she'd always said she'd take good care of Gail. All Melissa had to provide was the money.

Of course she hadn't been providing the money the last few months. But she couldn't help that. Wendy understood.

Wendy ought to understand.

Where could Gail be?

And what had Wendy done with the money, all that money?

She should never have agreed to the plan—never to know Wendy's new name or where she went—the money sent through Andie—

Six pairs of slacks. Six shirts. Four dresses. A couple of

skirts. That was all she could get into the suitcase. There was a bigger suitcase, but she wouldn't be able to carry it.

She slipped back out the door.

Sam's car still wasn't there. He might be somewhere along the beach; he'd acted like maybe he was looking for something.

Her car was a red GTO. She wished she had something less conspicuous, but there was nothing to do about it now. She pitched the suitcase into the seat, started the car, and left. Fast.

And only when she was back out on I-45 did she remember again that she didn't have anywhere to go.

Except—

Well, that was crazy.

But he wouldn't be back there tonight, anyway, that man who looked like Sam. She'd seen him carried to the ambulance; she wondered again, briefly, what had happened to him. But she thought of that only in passing, because right now she was too worried about herself.

If she still had the key Wendy had given her—given her laughing, saying, "I'm through with him, you want him now?"

She didn't want him. She didn't want anyone male, not ever again. But the house—

It was a place. Maybe, a safe place.

six

HE WOKE SLOWLY, LIKE A DAZED MAN COMing out of deep water, and for a moment everything was all right. Wendy was running water in the bathroom, and Gail must be still asleep, because he couldn't hear her and the television wasn't on.

"Shigata? Shigata, you got to wake up."

"Hunh? Al?"

"Yeah. Buddy, you got to wake up."

He sat, slowly. "Yeah. Gail?"

"Not yet. Here." A glass of cold water was slapped into his hand. He hadn't dreamed the running water, then. But it had been Al Quinn running the water, not Wendy, because Wendy was dead.

But not buried.

Not yet.

He supposed that was going to be his responsibility, but he didn't have time to think about it now.

He drank the water. Slowly, so as not to start retching again. "Nobody's found Gail?"

"Uh-huh. Here."

No lights. But clothes in his hand. Unfamiliar. Denim and chambray, from the feel. And his own gun belt. Quinn must have kept it last night.

"They'll probably be too short and too big around. But at least they're clean. Listen, Shigata, at eight o'clock there's gonna be about five Galveston cops out at your house to serve a search warrant."

"No Bayport cops?"

"Yeah. Me."

"So let them." He sat on the side of the bed, yawned deeply, and reached for the shirt he'd laid on the bed.

"I know. You can't stop them. But I figured you might like to be there when they get there. And at least be shaved and dressed."

"What if they don't want me there?"

"It's your house. And they don't have an arrest warrant."

He didn't add "Not yet." But it hung in the air. Shigata could hear it hanging there.

"What time is it?" he asked.

"Just after six."

The jeans were loose, but he tightened his own belt through the loops and they didn't feel too miserable. They were high-waters around his ankles, because he was maybe two or three inches taller than Quinn, but then he wouldn't have to wear them more than about half an hour.

The shirt was a little loose. But it was basically okay.

It was certainly better than putting his own clothes back on, after vomiting all over them. Especially in view of the fact that he hadn't the slightest idea where his own clothes were.

Daylight savings time was over. It was almost light when they got to his house, light enough that they could see a Galveston detective captain and a Galveston ident captain sitting in a beige sedan behind Shigata's car.

"Now what?" Quinn asked. His voice was quiet, but it held the same tone of anger Shigata had heard in it the night before.

"Now we play it by ear. *I* came home to take a shower and get on some clean clothes. *You* picked me up because we were ridin' together last night, and you knew I didn't have wheels at the hospital."

"Did I tell you what I told you?"

"They know you know?"

"Yeah."

"Then they know you told me, and there's no use lying about it. Al, they really think I killed Wendy, don't they?"

"Yeah. And that's not all."

"No?"

"Your daughter called that other killing in at six-twenty-three. That's for sure—it's on tape. But what she said was it happened 'a while ago.' No telling exactly what she meant by that, of course, and when the ME got hold of the body he said she died earlier than we guessed. More like about four, four-thirty. That say anything to you?"

"Oh hell," Shigata said. "Yeah. That says something."

"You left your office a little after two. You went to the League City Police Station to pick up some information one of their detectives had for you. You left there about three-fifteen. You didn't get back to your office until five-thirty. You stayed until seven-fifteen and left again. Three-fifteen until five-thirty. Time to get from League City to Bayport and back in to Houston. Plenty of time."

"Have you taken a warrant for me?" Shigata was surprised at how steady his voice was staying.

"No. I'm just telling you what it looks like."

"I drove from League City out to Clear Lake to talk to a possible witness to something. He wasn't at home. There wasn't anybody at his house. I stopped at a MacDonald's and got a hamburger. I dawdled over it because I was reading the new *Omni* and I knew I'd have to work late. You want to know the truth, I was goofing off."

"Can you prove it?"

"That's a dumb question."

"That's what I was afraid of."

"I called Gail from MacDonald's."

"Did you put it on your charge card? Or call collect?"

"Uh-huh. I dropped the little quarters in the little slot. But there must be some kind of record."

"Which it might be some kind of record."

"Which it might take a month to round up. But at least it's a little shred of alibi."

"Not really. I called at four-thirty. That could be on my way back to Houston."

"Shit."

"I'll bet they're wondering why we're just sitting here in the car."

"Or else they've guessed." His hand on the door handle, Quinn said, *"Shim-pai-nai."*

"Huh?" Shigata said.

"I said, *'Shim-pai-nai.'* "

"I heard you. What's it mean?"

His voice startled, Quinn said, "It's Japanese for 'Don't sweat it.' "

"Oh. Thanks. Only I don't speak Japanese."

They got out of the car. So did the Galveston officers. It was Shigata who said hello first.

"I guess you know why we're here." That was Captain Roy Hidalgo from CID. His voice was carefully neutral.

"Al told me."

"Want a look at the search warrant?"

"I've seen them before. I don't have anything to hide. Frankly, I'd like to take a shower while you search."

"Mind if one of us has a look in your bathroom before you start that shower?" His tone said he didn't care whether Shigata minded or not; he was going to have that look.

"Go ahead."

"Mind if one of us watches you take your shower?"

That, he could refuse. But refusal might precipitate his immediate arrest. And after they arrested him they could watch him do whatever they wanted to watch him do. "What do you think?" he asked bitterly.

"You're answering the questions."

"Yes. I mind. I mind a lot. Wouldn't you, if you were me?"

"Yeah," Captain Matthew Dean said. "But then, I'm not suspected of killing two women, either."

"And I am. I know it."

"Are you refusing?"

"Hell, no, I'm not refusing. You come right ahead and watch me take a shower. Want to watch me shit? Want to see if my asshole is slanted like my eyes?"

"Is it? Come off it, Shigata. I'm not liking this very much either."

Shigata stood in the bathroom and watched Matthew Dean search through his dirty clothes hamper, skim methodically through his medicine cabinet and linen closet, and then stand waiting.

Shigata began to undress. "The shirt and pants are Quinn's," he said conversationally. "Mine are still up at the hospital."

"No they're not. We got them last night. I noticed those didn't fit you so good. Thought they might be Quinn's." All the same, Dean felt around the collars and cuffs, turned all the pockets out.

With a carefully assumed appearance of quiet veiling his impotent fury, Shigata took off his undershirt and handed it over. It wasn't Dean's fault, he tried to tell himself; he knew evidence; he knew how it looked. But he couldn't help being furious, and Dean was the closest and so right now he was mad at Dean.

He knew Dean knew it.

But Dean didn't apologize. And maybe it would have been worse if he had.

He took off his jockey shorts and handed them over. Dean checked the waistband and crotch, and pitched them into the clothes hamper on top of the undershirt.

Shigata held his arms out away from his torso and slowly turned in a complete circle. He didn't ask Dean what he was looking for. He knew. He'd seen the broken fingernails on Wendy's body, too.

"Where'd you get the scrape?" Dean asked.

He knew Dean was going to ask that.

"I've been tearing down an old garage in the back yard," he said. He wondered how many times he'd said that in the last two days. "I got a little hasty and a board slipped and hit me."

"What shirt were you wearing?"

"I wasn't. It was hot. I was sweating."

"Can you prove that?"

"Yeah, sure, I always have people standing around to watch me tear down a garage, so they can provide an alibi when I'm accused of—" He took a deep breath. "No, I can't prove it. Gail might remember. When somebody finds Gail."

"If somebody finds Gail."

He looked up, quickly. "Dean, don't say—"

"I'm sorry." This time Dean did apologize. "Yeah. When somebody finds Gail."

He turned the shower on, adjusting the water to the right temperature.

Matthew Dean left the bathroom.

The search warrant was dated October 31. "That's Halloween," Shigata said aloud. "That's today."

"Yeah. Today's Halloween. Ho-ho-ho," Hidalgo said heavily.

"You mean trick-or-treat. Ho-ho-ho's for Christmas," Donna Gentry said, walking past him. She'd arrived while Shigata was in the shower, a fact he'd belatedly realized when he walked into his bedroom clad only in a dripping towel to find his bedroom occupied by a small redheaded woman busily engaged in searching through his dresser drawers.

She didn't seem particularly embarrassed, but she left.

He dressed, supervised by Matt Dean, in clothes she'd already examined.

Then he went to the living room to discover his boss Jim Barlow had arrived while he was dressing, and now was sitting in the recliner chair smoking a pipe. Barlow looked up as Shigata took his seat on the couch, but didn't say anything.

And Hidalgo had offered him the search warrant again. This time he accepted it, began to read it.

"Type AB blood?" he asked. "Why are you looking for something with type AB blood on it?"

"Your wife had type AB blood," Dean told him.

"No, she didn't."

"Oh, you've typed her blood yourself? How long ago was that?" Dean's sarcasm was somewhat overdone.

"No, but she *couldn't.* Last year when Gail had to have her appendix out her blood was typed, and she's type O. And a type AB mother *can't* have a type O child."

"Wouldn't that depend on the father's blood type?" Hidalgo asked doubtfully.

"Uh-uh," Donna said, pausing in the living room as Barlow turned silently to look at her. "He's right. A type AB mother can't have a type O child. She can have A or B or AB, depending on the father, but not O."

"Then they must have mistyped it."

"No they didn't," Shigata said positively. "There was some kind of complication and she had to have a transfusion. Gail's blood is type O. Period."

"Then they mistyped the victim's. Damn it, I *knew* I should have just said blood on the search warrant, instead of—"

"Oh no they didn't," Dean interrupted. "And if Doctor Morse heard you say that he'd spit green apples."

"But you said she was adopted," Quinn pointed out. "So what's the problem?"

"*I* adopted her," Shigata said. "I adopted her when I

married Wendy. But I've seen her birth certificate. It says mother, Wendy Collins, and it doesn't list a father. Look, she was born right out there at Mainland Center Hospital, six miles from here. Wendy grew up around here. That's why I asked to be transferred to Houston after Wendy and I were married in Denver—she said she still had a lot of close friends around here, and wanted to—"

"Have you got a phone somewhere besides the living room?" Dean interrupted, standing up.

"Yeah, in the bedroom."

"Hold on a minute. I want to check on something."

Nobody talked. They just waited, until Dean got back and said, "The hospital located the records. They show a Wendy Collins giving birth to a daughter named Gail, twelve years ago, all right. And according to them, both mother and daughter had blood type O. I'm going out to the hospital. Roy, you coming with me, or you want to wait here?"

"What are you going for?"

"They got a thumbprint of the mother and palmprints and footprints of the baby. Shigata, do you have—?"

"Gail's fingerprints? Yes, I took them years ago. I should already have given them—" They were in her baby book, in the bookcase in the living room. "School pictures," he added. "I've got the whole packet. They just came Thursday. I can—"

"I don't need any pictures right now," Dean said. "Just the prints. Yeah. Good clear ones, that'll help."

"I'll wait," Hidalgo said. "I'll wait right here."

"So the Wendy Collins who gave birth to Gail Collins isn't the Wendy Collins we found dead yesterday?" Captain Roy Hidalgo sounded pardonably confused.

"No." Captain Matthew Dean was being patient. "But the Gail that's missing definitely is the Gail who was born—"

"Then we don't have anybody's word but Shigata's that the body even *is*—"

"No, that's not right," Dean interrupted. "Wendy Collins has a record for prostitution that goes back to her seventeenth birthday."

"She what?" Shigata asked incredulously. "But she was in commercial sales! She told me—"

"You bet she was," Dean retorted. "And the Wendy Collins that was—in commercial sales, if you insist—is the Wendy Collins that married Mark Shigata—we can tell that by handwriting—and she's the Wendy Collins Shigata that's lying in the morgue today. And that still isn't all."

"What else, then?" Hidalgo asked.

"You know that right thumbprint of the phony Wendy Collins, the one that had the baby? Well, I've picked the same print up two places in the last two days."

"Where?" Hidalgo asked.

"In Wendy Shigata's bathroom. And in this kitchen, right here in this house. I don't know who she is. But she's been drinking coffee in this house. And I don't think it was very long ago. Because that was the only dirty coffee cup in the kitchen." He spun around in time to catch the puzzled look that passed between Shigata and Quinn. "What's with you two?"

"Just that we were both drinking coffee in the kitchen last night," Shigata said.

"And neither of us washed the cups," Quinn said.

"And nobody's supposed to have been in this house between the time I locked it up last night and the time I unlocked it this morning," Shigata added. "Not unless it was Gail."

"I don't know about Gail," Dean said. "But her mother was here. Gail's mother was here. Who's your girlfriend, Shigata?"

seven

"**I**'VE GOT TO PUT YOU ON ADMINISTRATIVE suspension until this is straightened out." Jim Barlow didn't say it unkindly, but his tone carried finality. "They haven't charged you yet. But they could. They've got about enough to write a warrant."

"Yes. I know. I went to law school, too, remember?"

"Mark."

"Yeah?" Shigata, sitting on the brown sofa, looked up at Barlow, who was standing by the front door.

"I've got to ask. Did you kill Wendy?"

"No." The voice stayed calm and steady.

"Did you kill that other one, the unidentified body?"

"No."

"Do you know who she was?"

"No."

"All right. I'm going on down to the Bayport Police Station to see what they've done so far on finding your daughter."

"*Is* she my daughter?" Shigata asked painfully. "I had

Wendy's consent for me to adopt her, but if Wendy didn't have the right—if Wendy wasn't really—''

"Right now, until a court says otherwise, it looks to me as if she's your daughter. And Mark. If you're on administrative suspension, I don't suppose the Bureau is going to be too interested in how you spend your time. Just so long as I can find you if I need to, I mean.''

"He'll be with me," Quinn said. "He'll be asleep or he'll be with me.''

"Tell me again who you are.''

Quinn sighed. Almost sighed. Didn't quite sigh. "Al Quinn. Bayport Police. I think I'm a detective.''

"You *think* you're a detective?''

"We had a lot of people quit and get fired. So they told me I was an acting detective. Right now we got an acting chief, an acting detective, and four patrolmen. Patrol officers. One of them's female.''

"Not acting patrolmen?''

"No. They're real patrolmen. Except two of them haven't been to training school yet. The chief's been a cop eighteen months.''

Jim Barlow closed his eyes momentarily. "And I've got a nineteen-year veteran whose career is riding on your investigation? Whose *life* may be riding on your investigation?''

" 'Fraid so," Quinn said equably.

"Mark, call me if I can help. But like it or not, I've still got an investigation of my own going on, the one you were on yesterday. I'll get the Bureau on your missing kid.''

What Al Quinn said about the Bureau, after the door was shut, wasn't excessively polite.

Mark Shigata didn't feel inclined to disagree.

"Y'know," he said, "right now I don't think I even *want* to be in the Bureau."

"Then quit."

"Nineteen and a half years—"

"So what? You don't like it, quit."

You don't like it, quit. That easy. That easy but he'd never thought of it. "Al?"

"Yo?" Al had his notebook out, was writing in his small, cramped handwriting.

"I'm not even sure I ever *did* want to be in the Bureau."

"Then why'd you do it?"

"I wanted to be a cop. So my dad said if I had to be a cop I should be the best. Get in the FBI."

"If your dad wanted somebody to be in the FBI, why didn't he—"

"Oh, he didn't. He was a lawyer. He wanted me to be a lawyer. So we compromised. I went to law school and I passed my bar exam and then I went to the Bureau."

"So what's the problem? You already told me your dad was flaky."

"I didn't say—"

"All right, you didn't, but what you said—"

"All right, so he was flaky. But—"

"Like I said, Shigata, my department needs a chief."

"They wouldn't have me."

Quinn shrugged. "You never know till you try. Okay? Here's what we've got to do. I've been thinking, and I—"

"We've got to find Gail, first. I feel like some more kind of a bastard, lying around at the hospital when God knows where Gail is."

"Shigata. Calm down. I wrote that down top priority.

Find Gail. And I've got some sources you Bureau boys never heard of."

"I kind of figured you did. Knowing the area and all."

"Okay. Second. We've got to find out who her natural mother is."

"Why's that second?"

"Because her mother showed up here—and we've got to find out why—and at Wendy's house. And I figure by the time we find out why she was at those other two places, we'll have done the other two things on my list."

"Which are?"

"Ident the corpse from your backyard. And find out who killed her and Wendy. That's bottom priority because we can't find it out until we find out the other stuff, and I figure once we find the other stuff out then we'll know that one."

"Quinn."

"Yeah?"

"Why are you so damn sure it wasn't me? I could have. You were right, I did have a motive, at least on Wendy. I don't know what my motive would have been on the other one. But I guess I could have had opportunity on both."

Quinn stood up. "I looked at you. That's why. I'm not an investigating computer, feed the facts in on one end and the answer comes out the other end. I'm a man. And you're a man. So I looked at you. I haven't got all the answers yet, not by a long shot. But the one answer I do have says that Mark Shigata's no killer."

"I think you're a better cop than I am, Quinn."

Al Quinn blushed easily; Shigata had noticed that before. He noticed it again as Quinn replied, "Well, mainly, I just pay a lot of attention to people."

Shigata had been on shrimp boats before. Maybe even on this one, though if he had he couldn't remember it. And he thought he would. This one was very clean, and it was painted a jarring bright blue. It smelled of fish. Not stale fish or rotten fish. Just fish. Clean white nets were spread neatly on the deck to dry.

Quinn shouted out what must be a greeting, although Shigata couldn't understand what he said, and then strode up the gangplank, talking rather loudly in what Shigata suddenly realized must be Vietnamese.

Vietnamese with a Texas drawl. It sounded funny. It looked funny, coming out of his ruddy weathered face.

A very short, lean man came out of the little cabin, grinning happily, and shouted an answer in a high-pitched singsong.

"Hoa, this is my friend Mark Shigata. My brother-in-law. Hoa. *Captain* Hoa." That last was punctuated with a grin.

"Hoa," the man said firmly. "Just Hoa. How-do-you-do, Mr. Shigata." A formal bow. Hoa's English was almost as high-pitched, as singsongy, as his Vietnamese.

Quinn went on talking; his Vietnamese must have sounded hilarious, although Hoa was clearly used to it. But Hoa's smile slowly faded, and he glanced at Shigata, his face eloquent of sympathy.

Quinn handed him one of Gail's school pictures.

Hoa looked at it, put it in his pocket. "I don't think she come here, Mr. Shigata. But if she come here, she be okay.

I tell my friends, okay, Al? You got some more pictures maybe?"

"I'll give you two more. Pass them around. Chances are, wherever she is, the kid's scared."

"Yeah," Hoa said. "I know about scared kids. We try to find her, yeah. But I don't think she come here."

They left him looking at the pictures.

"Where now?" Shigata asked in the car.

"The Cycle Shop."

"The what?"

"The Cycle Shop. Bikers."

"You intend to ask *bikers* to look for—?"

"You want her found, don't you?"

"Yes, but—"

"You want her found, you ask people who go places. Your Bureau, they go to clean places. They don't like to get their shoes dirty."

"Now that's not fair," Shigata objected. "I've gotten my shoes dirty plenty of times. Also my hands. And I've even got shot at a few times."

"Okay. I was exaggerating. But you know what I mean. They knock on doors and say, 'Have you seen this kid?' The Bandidos, they just go and look."

"Agreed, but what happens if they find her?"

"Nothing. They just let us know. She's a lady, ain't she?"

"She's twelve years old."

"Okay. But she's a lady. She ain't a punk."

"Oh. Yeah, I guess she's a lady. At least I've tried to get it across to her that she's supposed to be one."

"Bikers, they know the difference. They treat a lady like a lady."

Shigata's face expressed his doubt. But he didn't say anything.

There were three Bandidos at the Cycle Shop. They looked at the picture, looked at Shigata, looked at each other, and left with three of Gail's school pictures.

Five minutes later a bike paused beside the car at a stoplight. "Hey Quinn! Pull over!"

"Okay."

This biker was a big man, in a black sleeveless shirt. He had tattoos all over both arms, and an immense beer belly hung over a wide belt studded with bright metal. His long hair looked greasy, and he wasn't far short of Shigata's age. He wasted no time in greeting. "I seen your kid last night."

"Yeah?" Quinn said. "Where?"

"East Beach. About ten o'clock, maybe later. She was wearing—let's see. White pants. Awful dirty. Sneakers. I think they was pink. A dark blue jacket with a white stripe around each arm. She was carrying some kinda little blue satchel."

"Her gym bag," Shigata said. "East Beach, that's right beside—"

"She must've went to see—Oh lord," Quinn said. "I hope she couldn't get in—I hope—but that door was unlocked, she could have—"

"She went to see her mother," Shigata finished. "But where'd she go from there? And why—?"

"I ast her if she was lost," the biker said, "and she told me to go away. She was sitting in like a hole under the breakwater. I figured she was a runaway. But I figured it weren't none of my business. Kid that age, she'll go home when she gets hungry. I didn't know she'd seed no murder.'' He revved his motor.

"You want a five, Walker?" Quinn asked him.

"To look for a scared kid? Naah," Walker said. "If I see her again I'll call the pigs. She's scared of me."

"I don't blame her," Quinn said feelingly. "You looked in a mirror lately?" Walker laughed, revved his motor again, and was gone.

"East Beach," Shigata said. "We've got to—"

"Yeah," Quinn said, "but let's call the Beach Patrol and have them meet us there."

It had been a long walk. But she knew where she was going. It's hard to get lost in Galveston.

Gail was on Broadway. The road that I-45 turned into. Galveston's main drag.

She had bought a hamburger.

She was looking, wretchedly, at the change she had left from the five-dollar bill.

Supper tonight.

Lunch tomorrow.

That was all.

What then? What then? Where was there to go?

She ate the hamburger. And she cried.

Then, quite sensibly, she stopped crying and walked on over to the mall. She would be out of the wind there, anyway. She sat on a bench in the middle of the mall and coughed.

There wasn't anything else to do.

If she went to the health food store they'd give her a vitamin C and a spoonful of sunflower seeds. Or maybe they wouldn't. Maybe she was too dirty to go to the health food store.

A man sat down beside her, a young man with unruly light brown hair. He was wearing a yellow sweatshirt and he was eating cookies out of a bag. The cookies smelled good. They smelled like chocolate chip cookies.

He looked at her. He half smiled. Maybe he'd give her a cookie.

He didn't. He started reading a newspaper. She started to ask him for a cookie. He looked like a nice man. He'd probably give her one. But Daddy had told her it wasn't polite to beg, for crying out loud.

He put his newspaper down and walked away, leaving the rest of the cookies behind.

It wouldn't be stealing. He left them. It was like he threw them away. But all the same Gail waited until she saw him leave the mall before she ate them.

She was right. They were chocolate chip cookies.

She hoped he wouldn't remember where he left them. Maybe he wouldn't.

Idly, she glanced at the newspaper. And nearly screamed.

POLICE SEEK MISSING TEEN
ONLY WITNESS TO DOUBLE MURDER

That wasn't right. There was only one murder. Why did the newspaper think there were two?

There must be two, though. She'd gone back by that crummy house, and it now had a sign on the door. WARN-ING! CRIME SCENE! KEEP OUT! ORDERS OF THE GALVES-

TON POLICE DEPARTMENT. And there was yellow tape all around the door.

But she hadn't seen that murder. She didn't know why anybody would think she did.

But maybe that wasn't it. Maybe the police thought the same person did both of them. Maybe that was it. But they must not know who. If they knew who they would put it in the paper. Gail was sure of that.

She couldn't call Daddy. They might be listening in on the phone. She didn't know how that worked but sometimes she saw it on TV, people listening to other people's phones. If she called him they'd know where she was.

She wasn't scared he'd hurt her. That wasn't why she was hiding. She was hiding because she knew if they could find her they would make her tell what she'd seen.

And she couldn't.

She couldn't.

Daddy had told her never to lie. He'd said you had to tell the truth even if it wasn't pleasant. But she couldn't tell the truth. Not about this.

If she could just keep hiding long enough, she wouldn't have to tell a lie or the truth. Sooner or later they'd find out. She knew that. And, of course, she couldn't keep hiding forever.

But if somebody else told, if they found out some other way, it wouldn't be *her* that had told.

And then, quite suddenly, she realized. The man was reading this newspaper, with the picture of her right on the front page. And he'd kept looking at her, while he was reading.

The cookies. He'd left the cookies on purpose.

She ran.

*   *   *

"I swear, she was *right here!* I saw her and I *know* it was her! She looked—Well, she was filthy, nice white pants but grimy, I mean absolutely—"

"Yessir," the patrolman said wearily. This was the ninth person who'd reported seeing Gail Collins in the last half hour. She'd need roller skates. Or more likely a helicopter.

At least this one had the clothes right.

"Piggy dirty. And you could tell she was hungry, she kept watching me eat until I was ashamed of eating—"

You ought to be, thought the patrolman; the man was at least sixty pounds overweight.

"I'd have offered her some cookies, only I didn't want those grimy hands in the bag. And then I realized who she was. I figured if I started asking her questions she'd run, but I remembered the pay phones in front of the mall, and I thought—Damn, where'd she *go?* I'll bet it wasn't five minutes—Well, maybe ten, but no more—"

eight

"**I** TAKE ALL THE LITTLE KIDS TRICKIETREAT,"
Hoa announced.

"That's lotsa kids," Nguyen answered dubiously.
"Your kids, my kids, Huong's kids—"

"Yeah, lotsa kids," Hoa agreed happily. "You 'member
last year when I took all the kids to Astroworld?"

Nguyen shut her eyes momentarily. "I 'member," she
said. "I'm glad it was you paying for it and not me."

"Ah, money!" It was a very Gallic gesture. But then
Hoa had learned French before he'd learned English,
spent four years in school in Paris, and married a French-
woman. "What I care about money? There plenty of
shrimps in the Gulf. Lotsa little kids, though. So I need
the big kids too. Then the big kids can watch the little kids,
okay?"

"*All* the big kids? 'Cause I was gonna ask Johnnie to—"

"*All* the big kids," Hoa said firmly. "The big kids, the
little kids, I got *all* the kids today. You and Huong and
Natalie, you can take nap, yeah?"

"You got all the kids, me and Huong and Natalie can go to the mall."

"No, Natalie gonna take nap. She got the morning sick again."

Nguyen burst out laughing. "You're bad as Al."

"Ba-a-a-d," bleated Hoa enthusiastically, in imitation of someone his children had been imitating. His eyes were sparkling. "I got the kids, yeah? I bring the little kids home at eight, I keep the big kids. We stay on the boat. We goin' fishin' in the morning."

"Okay," Nguyen agreed resignedly. "You take the kids. And stay out of trouble!"

"Trouble? Me?"

Hoa was fifty-one. Sometimes he acted fifteen.

But he wasn't acting fifteen an hour later, sitting on the deck of the shrimp boat surrounded by twenty-three multilingual Asian and Eurasian children. "Now kids, here's what we gonna do—"

"The sign says authorized personnel only." Donna Gentry was leaning over the lower half of the double door to the identification office, both her hands draped casually across the top of it and pointing down at the sign.

"Dear Donna, sweet Donna, ain't I authorized?"

"Not so's I've noticed. 'Bye."

"Donna my girl, I need to look in your drawers."

"Whatcha looking for, a punch in the chops?"

"Your file drawers."

"Al, you know I can't—"

"Seriously. Sergeant Gentry—how's that? Donna, listen, the problem is I'm running into a dead end trying to get that corpse identified from Shigata's backyard and—"

"Dead end. Gaah, you didn't even say no pun intended."

"No pun intended. Sorry. Donna, kidding aside, okay?"

"Okay. But you know we already checked the fingerprint files. She wasn't in them. Not here, not in Houston, and we even wired Washington and—"

"I know that. So for pretty darn sure she's not on file anywhere, right? At least not by fingerprints."

"Okay, agreed, so what—?"

Mark Shigata wasn't used to standing idly while somebody else did all the talking. It bothered him. But at this moment, he was quite aware he had no official status. Except that of suspect, which he'd just as soon everybody would forget.

"Listen up and I'll tell you, okay?"

Shigata would never have used Al Quinn's method of asking questions. But they seemed to work for Quinn. He listened as Quinn went on. "We've got a definite link between the unknown and Wendy Shigata. Or at least pretty definite." Quinn did not look at Shigata when he said that. Gentry did, but her gaze, to Shigata's surprise, was devoid of accusation. It was merely assessing, and her eyes did not tell what judgment she rendered.

"Remember, that woman, whoever, Gail's mother, Wendy-two, went to both Wendy's house and Shigata's house. And it was *your* boss decided that. Fingerprint evidence. You can't get no better than that."

"So ask Shigata who she is."

"I don't know who she is." Shigata made his voice emotionless, a flat statement of fact. "She didn't go to the house when I was there."

"But what I'm thinking," Quinn said persuasively, "is, if we looked up Wendy's entire file with you, we could find out what companion cases she might have been arrested with—whether she ever listed any friends—who'd ever bonded her out—that sort of thing. And maybe one of those people will turn out to be our unknown. Or a link to our unknown, anyway."

"Oh," Gentry said blandly, "for that you need to go to records."

"Bitch," Quinn said between his teeth.

Shigata waited for fireworks.

Donna Gentry laughed.

"I'll call and tell 'em you cleared it with me," she added. "I don't think there's any supervisor in there this afternoon."

"Thanks." Quinn turned to head down the hall. "Nice girl," he added to Shigata. "I've known her about fifteen years. She used to come hang around the guard shack when she was trying to decide whether she wanted to be a cop or not. I taught her to classify fingerprints."

"You what?"

"I taught her to classify fingerprints."

Shigata glanced at the man beside him. "I refuse to ask."

The corners of Quinn's mouth were twitching. "Oilfield security I worked. Also refinery security. And the refinery was employing about six thousand people when I quit. See, it wasn't just a refinery, it was also a big petrochemical plant. And I would be chief of security if I was still there, which is part of the reason why I quit. An administrator I ain't. And don't want to be. I don't know how to play tough guy."

"So I noticed. But why in the hell did you let me think—"

"I let people think whatever they want to, until I start to get to know them. It's funny how much folks'll tell you, if they think you're too dumb to understand. You ought to try it sometime. I'll bet you've been so image conscious, with that great big chip on your shoulder, that you haven't even noticed your assets. And right now my ass is going to set right down here on this chair while sweet little Suzy-Q gets me that file I need."

"Sweet little Suzy-Q's ass is going to set right here at her desk until you ask properly," retorted a very large black woman who couldn't have been much short of sixty years old.

"Oh, Suzy-Q, Suzy-Q, you're going to have Shigata thinking you don't love me no more—Oh well, never mind. Suzy, this here's Mark Shigata. He's an FBI agent and I sorta think somebody's been tryin' real hard to frame him for murder. Now, I really do need the whole file on Wendy Collins, which is the former name of his late ex-wife."

"Hello, Sue," Shigata said when Quinn paused for breath. He'd met Sue Cook six months earlier. It had never crossed his mind to be anything but strictly business with her; he wasn't sure he'd ever seen her as a real person at all, and although she'd always gotten him what he asked her for, it had always been the bare minimum of what he asked for. She'd certainly never offered any extra information.

"Donna called and told me. Is the printout enough?" Sympathetic brown eyes rested for a moment on Shigata;

apparently she was seeing him as a person for the first time, too. "Or would you rather just borrow a terminal and—"

"I really need the old paper file, pre-computer, if you can find it. Is there any way—?"

"Well, yeah, I guess I can, but it'll take a while."

"We'll wait."

"I mean a *while.* Like about half an hour. Or maybe even an hour."

"No faster? Suzy, honest to God—"

"Al, I've got to look for it. That's really the best I can do. But I'll find it, I promise."

"Okay. If it's your best, it's your best. We'll come back. Bring you anything?"

"Uh-uh. Like what? Anyway, I don't need nothing."

"Shigata? You hungry?"

"I—" He hadn't thought about food. He couldn't remember when he'd thought about food. He'd eaten a hamburger at four o'clock on Friday. He'd been horribly sick at eleven that night. It was now one o'clock on Saturday. And he was ravenous.

Gail. What was Gail—?

Sometimes he thought Quinn must be able to read his mind. "You won't help Gail by starving yourself. She's resourceful. If she eluded that many people on the beach, she ain't going to go without food. She'll get it, one way or another. You know that's true."

Halloween.

That was the other thing she'd almost forgotten about. Halloween.

She hadn't gone trick-or-treating in years. Daddy wouldn't let her; he said it wasn't safe anymore. And of course, really, she was too old anyway. But people don't care, they might say something sarcastic to each other about the age of that kid, after they closed the door, but they'd hand out the candy and stuff all the same. She could find a group of kids and just tag along with them and nobody would pay her a bit of attention, and she'd get—

She'd get a lot of junk food, that's what she'd get. The kind of stuff Daddy wouldn't buy her, because he said it'd give her cavities and ruin her complexion and make her fat.

But it would be food.

Some people give apples and oranges, that's not junk food. And popcorn, that's cereal—well, sort of cereal. Popcorn balls. They're sweet and sticky, but they have cereal in them.

Or peanuts. Some people give peanuts. Daddy said peanuts have protein in them.

Some people even ask you in and give you hot chocolate. Not very many people, but some people do. Daddy did one year. Mom grumbled about it and said it made a lot of mess, but Daddy said it would be fun, and he let Gail ladle the hot chocolate out of the big punch bowl into the paper cups. After a while the hot chocolate started to get cool and he let her heat it up in the microwave. But then after it was hot he carried it back to the little table at the front door.

Halloween. The one day in all the year when it's okay to go and beg.

She'd have to get a sack. Well, that was easy, people were always throwing sacks away, and it didn't have to be a decorated sack. Or she could use her gym bag— Hey, that'd be perfect! She wouldn't have to worry then about even the heaviest apple tearing a hole in it, and of course she'd be wearing her jacket so there wouldn't be anything in the bag.

A costume. What could she do about a costume?

She sat down in a field by the police station to sort through her makeup—the makeup that was the reason she hadn't had quite so much of her saved-up lunch money left as she'd expected to have.

Let's see, she was certainly dirty enough, despite hurried washups in service-station restrooms, to look like a hobo. Some eyebrow pencil to make it look like her front teeth were gone. Her red headscarf, put on backward maybe, tied under the back of her neck instead of under her chin. Too bad it wasn't a bandanna.

It was too early now, of course, but she could plan just what to do.

Gail happily let herself be a child again.

A Bayport police car passed by. She didn't see it.

The two men in it, deciding where to go to lunch, weren't looking in her direction.

nine

HAMBURGERS ARE FAST.

But Quinn said they didn't have to be fast; Suzy had said an hour, hadn't she? And Shigata needed a good meal.

Shigata said he guessed so, but he didn't know Galveston that well.

Quinn said he knew a steak house where the detectives usually went to lunch.

"I don't want to," Shigata protested. "Look, eating lunch with somebody who thinks I'm a killer is not my idea of relaxing."

"Ah, it's late, they're probably through and gone anyway."

Shigata let himself be persuaded.

And regretted it when he saw two captains sitting over bowls of salad, waiting for their steaks to arrive. Quinn blandly strolled over to the table and sat down with them.

Both captains looked uninvitingly at Shigata.

Feeling ridiculously self-conscious, he sat down too.

"Well!" Quinn beamed, unfolding his paper napkin.

"What a coincidence, you two being here just when we happened to arrive."

"Yeah," Hidalgo said heavily. "What a coincidence. I assume it was your idea." Hidalgo was a big man, probably six-four, over two hundred fifty pounds, and today he wasn't wearing his bulk well. It was weighting him down.

"Believe me, it wasn't my idea." Shigata began to butter a cracker. He ate it and buttered another one.

"You always eat butter on your crackers?" Hidalgo asked him.

"Yeah. Why?"

"Just wondered. I do too. Have another cracker." He waved vaguely in the direction of the cracker basket.

"Thanks."

Shigata did not know how to make dinner-table conversation with people who were accusing him of murder. Apparently Dean and Hidalgo did not know how to make dinner-table conversation with someone they were accusing of murder.

It was quite astonishing how silent a large room with four men in it could get. Even the waitress was quiet, sitting in a chair beside the tea urn, filing her fingernails and studiously looking away from her customers.

Quinn ate his salad. Noisily.

Dean and Hidalgo looked at each other.

"You taken a warrant yet?" Quinn asked, unnecessarily rattling his salad plate.

Hidalgo and Dean looked at each other.

Shigata looked at his cracker. He began to spread more butter on it. It broke. He wiped the butter off his hand with a paper napkin.

"No," Hidalgo said. "We haven't taken a warrant yet."

"That's good," Quinn said.

"Number fourteen," the loudspeaker said. "Where's number fourteen?"

"That's us," Hidalgo said. Dean raised his hand. The waitress put her nailfile in her pocket.

"Why is that good?" Dean asked.

"That's good because Shigata gets to eat his dinner without being arrested." Quinn bit a carrot stick. Crunched it. "Are you going to take a warrant?" he asked.

"Not at the moment," Dean said.

Quinn reached for a piece of celery. "That's good," he said.

"The celery, or the warrant we haven't taken yet?" Hidalgo asked.

"Well, if you don't take a warrant you don't serve it," Quinn said. He buttered a cracker. "So maybe Shigata eats supper too."

"I think I'm losing my appetite," Shigata said.

"Too many crackers," Quinn told him. He gulped ice tea, signaled the waitress, and pointed at his glass.

Dean began to cut his rib eye. Hidalgo, who'd ordered the pepper steak, asked for soy sauce.

"Why soy sauce?" Shigata asked him.

"I like it on my baked potato," Hidalgo said. "Why?"

Shigata shook his head, and the loudspeaker said, "Number fifteen. Where's number fifteen?"

Quinn raised his hand. "Shigata," he asked a moment later, talking around a mouthful of baked potato, "did Wendy have any sisters?"

"She said she didn't. But after what I've learned about her yesterday and today, I don't know what that's worth."

"Yesterday?" Hidalgo said. "What did you learn about her yesterday?"

"You want to give him his rights again?" Quinn asked.

"Shut up, Quinn," Hidalgo said. "What did you learn about her yesterday, Shigata? That she was a whore? Or did you learn that—say—Tuesday? Or maybe Wednesday? When did you learn your wife was a whore?"

"I learned a month before she moved out. At least—"

"At least what?"

"At least that she was doing it, not that she was getting paid for it."

"How did you learn that?" Hidalgo asked. "That she was doing it?"

Shigata looked at his plate, stabbed at his French fries.

"I said, how did you learn that, Shigata?"

"I learned it when I put my arms around her and smelled another man's aftershave in her hair. Musk. And I've never used musk in my life. Now shut up and let me eat my dinner, damn you."

Hidalgo looked at Dean. Dean looked at the table.

"That didn't happen last Tuesday," Quinn said softly. "You don't wait seven months to kill for something like that."

"What did you do then?" Hidalgo asked. "You don't have to answer that. It's just that I don't know what the hell I'd do if it was me."

"I didn't do anything," Shigata said. "Not anything at all. Because—because I kept hoping. I kept hoping she'd settle down and so I pretended not to know. Doesn't that make any sense to you, that I'd just—pretend I didn't know? But it went on. It went on. And finally I quit caring. Or thought I did. And that's what I learned last night. That

I still cared. I thought I didn't, but I did. Seeing her—last night—the way she was—I still cared."

Hidalgo finished his steak. Then he said, "Shigata. I can't play personalities. I can't play hunches. Fact—She was your wife, not your ex-wife. Fact—She was a whore, and you knew it. Fact—She was still asking you for money."

"How do you know that?" He didn't look at Quinn.

"She kept a diary."

"A diary?" Quinn asked sharply.

"Yeah," Shigata said. "I forgot about that. She kept—it wasn't a real diary. It was Avon, of all things. It was like one of those book-style business calendars, the kind you use to keep track of appointments and that kind of thing. Let's see, last year's had a rose on it. I think this year's had some kind of Victorian lady on the front of it."

"Funny the killer didn't take that," Quinn said. "Must mean the killer didn't know about it."

"Or else the killer forgot about it," Dean countered.

Hidalgo continued. "Fact—She was threatening to take her daughter, to take Gail away from you."

"Not fact," Shigata said.

"Diary says so."

"Then she lied to the diary. She never said one word to me about wanting Gail. She hadn't even *seen* Gail but twice since she left."

Hidalgo and Dean looked at each other. "It didn't actually say *Mark,"* Dean admitted unwillingly. "It said *M.* Just the initial *M.* Let's see—'Tell M to pay up or—' What was the rest of it, Roy? I don't remember."

" 'Tell M to pay up or kid goes back.' "

"Kid *goes* back?" Shigata repeated. "Wouldn't that be

more likely to say *comes* back if she meant she was taking Gail back?"

"Then what do you think it means?"

Shigata shook his head. "I don't know what it means. But I know what it doesn't mean. She hadn't made any such threat to me. And if she had I wouldn't have killed her. I'd have gotten a lawyer and probably hired some detectives and fought her every way I could, but I wouldn't have killed her. Anyway, not if there was anything else left to do I wouldn't."

Hidalgo lit a cigarette.

Shigata put down his fork. "The two of you are sitting there so sure I killed her you're not looking at anything else. You searched the house, right? Her house?"

Dean forked a piece of pecan pie. "Of course."

"I'm asking you to do two things. I know you don't have to do either one. But in the name of common humanity—realizing as I think you do that I've been a law enforcement officer for over nineteen years, and I've never before in my life been suspected of going off the track even for a second—at least hear me out. First, let me go through what you found there and brought in. Something might say something to me when it wouldn't to you, because I knew her—or I lived with her. Maybe I didn't really know her, but I thought I did. Then, let me go back over to that house and search it again myself. I'm not asking you to leave me alone with any part of it. Don't leave me alone—one of you stay with me every minute. Watch everything I do. You have to do that. Because I know what the evidence looks like. You don't have to tell me. I know you could get an indictment right now. Maybe you could even get a conviction right now. But gentlemen, I didn't do it.

•

And I don't think either one of you wants to convict an innocent man."

There was a long silence.

"We shouldn't," Hidalgo said.

"Him seeing the evidence isn't going to change the evidence," Dean pointed out.

"If you'll stay with him in the property room, I'll take him out to the house." Hidalgo downed the last of his tea and stood up. "PD in ten minutes."

"We'll be there," Quinn said. "Shigata, while you're doing that, I'll round up those names we talked about. We can work on that later this afternoon."

"Right," Shigata said.

He felt a little like a cop again.

Just a little.

But it helped.

ten

ASK ANY IDENT TECH. THEY'LL ALL AGREE.
Ident gets the broom closet.

Only not in Galveston.

It was a large, well-lighted suite of rooms, with latent processing area, work desks, and photo lab conveniently near each other. Too small for the twelve people who worked in it, of course, but ident is always too small. Certainly better than most Shigata had seen.

He was sitting in front of Matthew Dean's desk, watching Dean take evidence bags out of a cardboard box and take items of evidence out of the bags.

Pieces of a broken lamp. "It came with the house," Dean said. "We've established that. No prints on it. And nothing else. She wasn't hit with it. Somebody just knocked it over during the struggle. Funny though, it was clear over by the back window of the bedroom, and there's no other signs they were fighting over there."

A coffee cup. "That's what whoever it is left her fingerprints on. In the bathroom, of all places, like she'd gone in and seen the body and left the cup then. It had bourbon in it, not coffee, by the way. And we didn't find the bourbon bottle in the house. Scotch, not bourbon."

"And that's the same 'her' that left fingerprints at my place?"

Dean nodded. "Same one. So who is she?"

"Quinn calls her Wendy-two," Shigata said. "I guess that's as good as anything else until we find out who she was."

"Was?"

"Is. Whatever."

"Why'd you say was? You think she's dead too?"

"I don't know why I said was. I just did, that's all. I haven't the faintest idea whether she's dead too. How could I when I don't know who she is? What else?"

A candle. One of her collection. Wendy collected candles. She didn't burn them. The killer didn't know that. Shigata told Dean, and Dean said, "Well, it was burning. In the kitchen. Right next to a stove burner on full with the pilot light out. Too bad the killer didn't notice the busted window pane over the sink. Too bad for the killer, anyway. Because the gas got out the window and the fire never started. The candle eventually blew out."

"Then that's why—"

"Why what, Shigata? Why the fire didn't start? How come you asked Quinn if the gas was out? How'd you know it was on?"

"I smelled it." Keep your temper, he told himself. Keep your temper. Keep your temper. "Okay, yes, I smelled the gas. But anyhow he had to have been planning to burn the house. Why else did he put her in the bathtub? Accidental drownings don't leave blood all over the bedroom wall. They don't break necks. They don't leave the kind of marks she had on her throat. You don't have to be in the FBI to know somebody planned a fire, Dean, and you don't have to be a killer. And yes, I know anything I say may be used against me. You want me to sign a Miranda form, I'll sign it. And then I'll say it again. Yes. I wondered why the place wasn't burned. But I'll tell you something else, Dean. I'm not stupid. And because I'm not stupid, if I was planning to make it look like fire I'd leave her in the bed, not in the bathtub. So whoever did it was stupid. Bathrooms don't burn so well."

"Maybe he was stupid. Or maybe he wanted us to think he was stupid. And maybe he was working a triple bluff."

"Maybe," Shigata said evenly. "What else did you find?"

"You aren't lacking for guts, anyway," Dean said in a half-amused, half-exasperated tone. "Okay. This."

The diary. It had an Edwardian lady on the front and pretty sepia-toned fin de siècle pictures in it. Notes on nearly every day through October 27. Notes in pencil, notes in blue ink, notes in black ink. Appointments, memos. Names with figures after them. Telephone numbers followed by dollar signs followed by names. Always men's names. Motel room numbers, sums beside them. Sums added up, mostly wrong. Those elegant, conventional Edwardian ladies illustrated what was indisputably the diary of a whore.

"Mind if I make a photocopy?" Shigata asked.

Dean looked at him, then shrugged. "No. Go ahead. That's basically all, anyway. You don't need to see the biological samples."

It was a statement, not a question, but Shigata shook his head.

"Or the lifted latents."

"No." The identification section of the Galveston Police Department was probably the best in the state; any idents they couldn't make couldn't be made. "Were any of the prints mine?"

"Have I printed you for comparison?"

"No. I figured you'd gotten them from the Bureau."

"I didn't. And I can't require you to be printed. You haven't been charged with anything. Are you volunteering?"

"I'm volunteering."

The ink slab wasn't the usual rectangle of glass bolted to the counter; instead, it was a thick disk on some kind of axle that allowed it to spin freely. A standard fingerprint card, the touch pads of all ten fingers, both rolled and dabbed. Major case prints, the full length, sides, and tips of all ten fingers. Palm prints, both flat and curved sides. Dean was thorough. And neat.

He sat down with an envelope of lifted latents, precisely taped onto properly labeled small white cards.

It took him ten minutes to make the comparisons.

Shigata, waiting, cleaned the ink off his hands with lanolin, went and washed the lanolin off in the men's room, and returned to begin reading the diary.

Dean put his magnifier down. "No. None are yours. You knew that, though, didn't you?"

"Not really. I knew I hadn't handled anything in the bedroom or bathroom or that little kitchen area. But I hadn't the faintest idea what I might have touched in the living room when I started flaking out."

"What the hell happened to you, anyway? I thought for sure you were having a heart attack."

Shigata shrugged. "I heard one of the EMT's say shock. That's all I know. You don't have anything else from the scene?"

"Uh-uh. As I said, that's it."

"No murder weapon?"

"Somebody's hands. For sure. I went to see the autopsy. You want to hear about it?"

Shigata wasn't at all sure he wanted to hear about it. But he knew he had to. Either now or in a courtroom. "Yeah. Tell me about it."

"Crushed hyoid. Two crushed cervical vertebrae. Broken neck, in other words. As you guessed. Manual bruising even more pronounced inside the skin than on the surface. Somebody didn't like that chick, and that's a fact."

"You get measurements of the hands?"

"Too distorted. But he's got strong fingernails. You can see the impressions of them inside the skin of the neck." Dean looked pointedly at Shigata's hands, now crossed over the diary.

Shigata didn't move. "Yes. I've got strong fingernails. As do quite a few other men in southeast Texas. Go on."

"No water in her lungs at all. She was positively dead before she got put in the bathtub."

"What about the wound on the side of the head? I never did get much of a look at it."

"Photos, if you can handle seeing them. I don't want anybody barfing on my desk."

"I can handle seeing them."

It's only a corpse. It's only a crime scene.

Not Wendy. Not Wendy clowning with a towel covering her wet hair, pretending to be a swami; not Wendy, walking through the bedroom in high-heeled rhinestone sandals and rhinestone earrings and nothing else, wiggling her bottom at her new husband and giggling.

Not Wendy, totally bewitching a naive, trusting man with whore's tricks she must have used a million times before.

Only a crime scene.

Only a dead woman, several days dead, out of the bathtub now and lying on a stretcher with someone holding the right side of her head to demonstrate an ugly gaping wound that exposed part of the cheekbone and jaw.

"Somebody hit her with something," Dean said unnecessarily.

"I sort of guessed that. But what?"

"Now, I was hoping you might help me with that."

"I can't think of anything that would make that kind of wound."

"Maybe the edge of a lead-weighted sap? Like this one maybe?" Shigata didn't see where it had come from, only that Dean was now hefting it, demonstrating its spring, its weight. It was small, black, well-worn, and deadly.

"Where'd you get that?"

"Out of your bedroom."

"I've never owned such a thing in my life. Where in my bedroom?"

"Look at your copy of the search warrant. I gather you didn't read it. We provided you an inventory of everything we took. Including this."

" That's not mine and I never saw it before. And the warrant is at home. You're right, I didn't read it. Just tell me."

"The sap was shoved between the bedsprings and the mattress on the right-hand side of your bed, right where you could get at it without getting out of bed."

"I didn't put it there."

"You haven't changed the sheets since Wendy left?"

"I change the sheets every week. Almost every week. And I don't think that was Wendy's, either. I think—I don't think she started out to cheat on me. I think she started out, well, not loving me, but at least liking me. She'd have showed it to me to see what I thought about it, if she'd had it when we got married. And after she left, I spread out to both dressers, both closets. That room is small. I'd have found it. And I damn sure would have found it if I was sleeping on it."

"Then where'd it come from, do you think?" Dean slapped it softly down in the palm of his left hand. Not softly enough. He winced and whistled.

"Wendy-two, maybe?"

"Who?"

"Whoever. The fake Wendy. The fingerprint on the cup. Gail's—mother. I didn't spend last night in that house. Maybe she did. Maybe she left it."

Dean toyed with the sap. "How'd she get in? No sign of forced entry. You've got good locks on that house."

"I put good locks on that house. I seem to have offended the KKK. And I don't know how she got in. But you know she did."

"That was no KKK killing, not Wendy, not that woman behind your house. The KKK does a lot of things, but they don't usually mess with women. At least not white women. Maybe you gave her a key. Whoever she is."

"I've told you already I didn't give her a key and I don't know who she is."

"If you were sitting where I'm sitting would you believe what I'm hearing?"

"You've got a polygraph. You know how to use it."

"Polygraphs can be beaten. You're smart enough to know how. No. There's no blood on the sap, if that's what you were getting ready to ask. Not even in the seams. I don't think it was the murder weapon. If it was, it was enclosed in something, like a plastic bag, and I don't really think that's likely. But something like that. Or a baton."

"Sorry, I don't own a baton, either." Quinn would call a baton a billy-club. But whatever you wanted to call it, Shigata didn't own one.

"Or maybe one side of a set of numchucks."

Nunchako, Shigata mentally corrected, but didn't say anything.

"Or even the butt end of a whip, but I can't see anybody taking a whip in there. That's all, Shigata. We didn't collect much at the scene. There wasn't much at the scene that had anything to do with the case. The killer cleaned up after himself real good. Damn good, considering he was planning a fire." Dean stood up. "I'll take you to Hidalgo. But I'm telling you in all honesty, and I wouldn't want to lie to you because you and me go back at least a little ways, if things don't change we're going to have to take a warrant for you in the next few days. And if we do, the DA's office is going to order Quinn to take one, too. And it wouldn't do him any good to refuse."

"I know. They're down to six men already, what would one less matter?"

"Precisely."

"Which way's Hidalgo's office? I always get turned around in this building."

"I'll show you."

Dean was right.

There wasn't much at the house that had anything to do with the case. And what there was, Dean had already collected.

He should have known. Galveston has a good identification section. He'd asked for their assistance enough times himself.

The car was parked on the beach, where they could see any twelve-year-old girls that might happen to pass by. Only none did. The sun was sparkling on the water and the sand looked cleanswept except for the washed-up hulks of jellyfish that looked like clear plastic models. The car doors were open and a breeze was blowing through, riffling the papers Quinn was holding.

"Arrested February 'sixty-seven, prostitution. Suspended sentence. Arrested April 'sixty-seven. Street walking on Post Office Street. Nul prossed for lack of evidence. Arrested July 'sixty-nine, prostitution, probated sentence. September 'sixty-nine, drunk, paid a fine. January 'seventy, drunk and fighting, fined. March 'seventy, prostitution. March 'seventy again, prostitution. That's two arrests a week apart, and she got six months to serve. November 'seventy, prostitution. Probated sentence. July 'seventy-one, possession of marijuana, nul prossed. September 'seventy-three, prostitution."

"Wonder why the lull?" Shigata asked.

"Attached rap sheet shows four arrests in the interim

around the Dallas–Fort Worth area. Anyhow. Four arrests in 'seventy-five, more of the same. Last one in November of 'seventy-six. Not a nice girl, your Wendy."

"I suppose it stopped after that because she moved away."

"No, apparently not." Quinn unfolded another sheet of paper. "I walked over to the library and had a look at the city directories. She was living on Avenue O in Galveston until 1977."

"She told me she moved to Denver in July of 'seventy-seven. Gail would have been eighteen months old then."

"How did she live in Denver? I mean money, source of income?"

"She told me she was in commercial sales. She wasn't doing well at it. She wasn't living very well. I don't think she was whoring then, Al."

"Maybe not. Maybe not. But—you never knew her to do dope? Because if she was whoring and doing dope she could be living damn low on the hog even with a lot of money."

"I never knew her to. But of course I've had to work nights some, be out of town some. I'd have known if she'd had a habit. But I wouldn't necessarily know if she'd done just a little pot, a little speed, a little coke, while I was out of pocket, just so long as she didn't leave it lying around. I'd have spotted it if she'd done that, of course."

"What was she selling? She was in commercial sales, she had to be selling something."

"For a while it was pantyhose. She kept a L'eggs van parked in her driveway. But she said she didn't like it, she really didn't understand the job and she hated to get out in bad weather. It didn't last long. After that, cosmetics.

Avon, Mary Kay, something else. She didn't stay with anything long."

"Since when are Avon and Mary Kay commercial sales?"

"Sales, anyway. I tried to help her figure a few profit-and-loss sheets. It was hopeless. She didn't know what they were."

"Well, anyway, since this record was so old, I checked with the Bureau and had them wire me an updated rap sheet on her. Nothing after nineteen seventy-seven. You married her when, did you say?"

"November nineteen eighty-three."

"Six years. She wasn't whoring, or she'd have gotten caught. Her record makes that pretty clear. She wasn't subtle—she couldn't have been, to get caught that many times, and she wouldn't have changed unless somebody smart was running her. I hate to ask it, but what about after you were married?"

"Nobody was running her. We moved a lot the first few years, and she didn't have any unexpected absences until that last six or seven months. She wasn't whoring."

"But she supported herself and a child—not even her own child—for nearly six years, in commercial sales, when she couldn't even make out a profit-and-loss sheet? And you said yourself she didn't have any kind of a head for business. Come on, Shigata. What was she living on for those six years? Why did she suddenly go back to the old way of life—how long ago?"

"Looking back on it, I guess about this time last year. Because it was about six months ago she left, and it was about six months before, that she started acting so—so mysterious. But I don't know why, Al. I wasn't keeping her short of money any more than I could help. I mean I kept out twenty a week for my lunches and gasoline—which wasn't always enough—and I gave her the rest, at least I did until she quit paying the bills and started buying clothes with the utility money. She wanted us to eat out all the time. For some reason she had it in her head it was cheaper. And then one time I got the checkbook and went to pay the electric bill, because they were threatening to cut us off, and I couldn't because she'd already spent the money for a pair of boots. I had to call the credit union to get the money."

Once he had started talking, it seemed he couldn't stop; old resentments poured out. "It was like she couldn't tell the difference between need and want. Finally I took all the bill paying back and put her on an allowance, and even that didn't work. I remember one time we were so darn broke we couldn't afford a new needle for the stereo. Now, that is pretty darn broke, right? And for some reason or other I had to work Saturday afternoon, and she came up to the office to show me what she'd done. She'd bought a new stereo. On credit. And she was so proud of herself, she thought she'd done something really smart. I remember she said, 'But Mark, we need it! The old one was all worn out.' "

"Ouch," Quinn said.

"Yeah. Ouch. But as to before we were married, I don't know, Al. I—you're in love, you don't ask the woman how she's supporting herself. She was doing a piss-poor job of it, I can tell you that. Gail didn't have a winter coat. November in Denver, and Gail didn't have a winter coat. We went from the wedding chapel to Sears."

"I'll bet Wendy had a winter coat."

"Yeah. She did. But she said she got it at Goodwill."

"Oh, Goodwill's stopped stocking kid's coats?"

"Can it, Al. You've made your point, and I wasn't arguing anyway. What did you get on names?"

"A half sister. Andrea Collins."

"Who could have used her sister's name to have a baby."

"Could have," Quinn agreed, "but why would she?"

"Why would anybody? I think if we knew that we'd just about have this case cleared up."

"True. Okay, a stepsister, Melissa Blair."

"Go on."

"A friend. Jack Heyer. For friend you can probably read pimp. He bailed her out six times."

"Okay. Wonder if she'd gone back to work for him?" He made his voice impersonal. She. A victim. Not Wendy. A person. A defense mechanism. If you don't say the person's name you can almost—sometimes—keep the person a non-person even if it is somebody you know.

And your victim has to stay a non-person. You can't investigate when you're crying.

"We'll need to find out," Al was saying.

"Any others?"

"That's all."

"We got addresses?"

"We got old addresses. Very old. When Barlow put you on suspension, did he take your ID away from you?"

"Uh-uh."

"That's good. My badge is worth damn-all in Galveston, and I'd just as soon keep the Galveston PD out of it."

"I'll get my tail in a sling for sure."

"Which is worse, your tail in a sling or a needle in your arm up in Huntsville?"

"Let's go ask questions." Shigata closed his car door. "You sure it was Gail that man saw in the mall?"

"The clothing description matches yours. And he picked her picture out."

"And she looked okay except for being dirty?"

"If you call a hamburger, a Coke, and a sack of chocolate chip cookies okay. It's like that Bandido said, Shigata. She gets hungry enough, she'll go home. She ain't a stupid kid."

eleven

"**A**L?"

"Yeah?"

"I've worried the shit out of you about Gail, haven't I?"

Quinn glanced at him. "Yeah. But that's okay. If she was mine I'd be half crazy. A girl, that young, gone missing. My head says she's okay. But my stomach don't like it."

"Would you feel like telling me about your boy?"

There was a long silence. "About Mark," Quinn said finally. "Yeah. Mark was sixteen. He wanted to go to that big Scout thing, the national jamboree. I told him I'd like him to go but there was just no way I could come up with enough money. He understood that, he—Mark was a good boy. All my kids are good kids. I told him if he'd raise half of it doing lawn work and that kind of thing I'd come up with the rest of if I had to borrow it. He said no, he wanted to earn it all. He said he guessed he needed about a thousand dollars. He worked after school, he worked on weekends. When he died, in April, he had nine hundred and seventy-five dollars in the bank and twenty-five in his pocket. He'd have been able to go. I—we gave the money to his Scout troop. Told them to send somebody. He—I told you he was hit by a car. It was just after dark, and he was walking home in dark clothes. We never even found out where he'd been working that day. The car never stopped. It knocked him around pretty bad—he wasn't even recognizable, and his jacket never did turn up. He was a good boy." Quinn blinked. "He was a good boy."

"Sounds like it. I'm sorry, Al. I don't think I said that earlier."

"Yeah," Quinn said, "yeah, well, you do what you can. Is this the address we had on Heyer?"

"This is it."

It wasn't a pimp's house.

Jack Heyer was fat. Enormously fat, and his hairless chest, which was immediately visible because he was wearing no shirt, needed a bra. If they make size 50E bras, Shigata thought, gazing at him in fastidious horror.

He was shoeless. His toenails were grimy claws he undoubtedly could not reach to cut, and his stubby toes were otherwise almost invisible in feet too fat for most shoes.

He was wearing khaki pants, and apparently, nothing else.

His legs moved from side to side, rather than directly in front of him, and the rolls of fat on his abdomen shifted and the rickety staircase shook as he walked down from the unpainted front porch to stand on the sidewalk, arms akimbo because they couldn't hang down beside him.

"Cops," he said. "Jeez. What've I done now?"

"Nothing right now," Quinn said. "We just want to talk to you." His tone was not noticeably friendly.

"Yeah? Well, what kind of cop are you? Got a name?"

"Al Quinn. Bayport Police."

"I got news for you, piglet. This is Galveston."

Quinn glanced at Shigata, who obligingly pulled his own identification out. "Mark Shigata. Federal Bureau of Investigation. And last time I heard, Galveston was still in the United States, right?"

"Shigata!"

"The name mean something to you, punk?" Quinn said.

"No. Why should it?"

"Like maybe Wendy Shigata? Used to be Wendy Collins? You running her, man?" Quinn was crowding into Heyer's space, and Heyer backed up a step.

But he recovered fast. "Who're you calling a pimp? You some kind of a nut?"

"Quinn, settle down," Shigata said in a too-patient tone of voice. "I told you you were imagining things. Mr. Heyer was an old friend of Wendy's, that's all."

"Friend, pah!" Quinn spat on the sidewalk.

"That's right," Heyer smirked, "me and Wendy was friends, back ten, fifteen, years ago, that's all. Sure I was glad to see her back in town, 'cause we's friends. You just got a nasty mind, Quinn."

"Sure, and you got her out of jail because you were such a good friend, right?" Heyer started to nod, and Quinn added, "What'd she thank you with, cash or ass?"

"Now look—"

"Whose was the baby, Heyer? Yours?"

"Baby! Wendy didn't have no baby!"

"Quinn, if you'll just settle down. You're asking everything all wrong and you're getting Mr. Heyer all riled up and it's just not necessary." Heyer smiled ingratiatingly, hopefully, as Shigata went on, "Mr. Heyer, we know Wendy didn't have a baby herself. But she was taking care of one. Did you know about that?"

A series of emotions raced across Heyer's face; evidently, he was trying to decide what answer to that question would be least likely to be incriminating. Finally, warily, he said, "Yeah. Yeah, I know about that."

"You know whose baby it was?"

He looked vague. "Should I know?"

"Wendy's dead, bastard!" Quinn shouted. "And some other broad we haven't even identified yet is dead too, and you're gonna help us find out who killed her. Or would you rather get run in on suspicion yourself? That'd put a crimp in your pimping business, wouldn't it?"

The days of running people in on suspicion were long gone. But Heyer probably didn't know that.

"Shut up," Shigata said quickly. He'd been gauging Heyer's reactions while Quinn was playacting, and the bad-cop routine had gone sour. Shutters had closed down behind the calculating eyes.

"I don't know nothing," Heyer said. "Not nothing. No. I don't know whose the baby was. And listen, I told you I ain't no pimp. Somebody give me the money to get her out of jail."

"Somebody like who?"

"I dunno. It come in the mail."

That wasn't impossible, just somewhat improbable.

Shigata took a deep breath. "Look," he said, "I think we've gotten off on the wrong track. We're upset, and we've got you upset too."

Heyer didn't answer. He stared at Shigata, and there was fear in his eyes.

"What happened ten, twelve, fourteen years ago, that's not what matters now. We need to know who the mother of the child is, the real mother, because whoever killed Wendy and that other woman might be wanting to kill her too. We need to know who was running Wendy, because he might be the killer. We're not accusing you of anything. We just want you to help. Can you do that?"

"You might not be accusing him of anything, but *I*—"

"Quinn. That's enough. He's not a pimp. You can tell that by looking at him."

That was perfectly true. Any whore in any town, looking at Heyer, would be convulsed with laughter, not with fear. Quinn, realizing all that, turned his head not quite fast enough to hide a grin.

Heyer looked puzzled. "How can you tell that? I mean, I'm not, but—"

"I'm a good judge of character," Shigata said, and Quinn wiped his hand across his mouth, trying to hide another grin.

"Well—okay, you say so. Honest to God, I don't know who the baby belonged to. Wendy just showed up with it one day and said she'd landed a cushy job. She said she was tired of all the pricks what *was* pricks. She said she'd play when she wanted to play, and no other time."

"And did she?"

"Did she what?"

"Play. Did Wendy go on playing?"

"Oh yeah. Just not so much. Like she said, she played when she wanted to play."

"She ever play with you?" Quinn asked.

"Me?" Heyer contemplated his belly. "I look like a classy dame would play with me?"

"Okay. So she moved away finally. She showed back up—when?"

"About a year ago. See, Alton, that bookie, he used to run her. I mean that's what got her started to begin with, she needed the money to pay him. Alton's been around about a hunnerd years I guess. And he was still around when she come back to town."

Quinn and Shigata looked at each other. Neither of them had guessed gambling.

"So when she come back—I don't know just exactly when that was, maybe about a year or so ago—she was placing bets with Alton. And she was paying off just fine and seemed to have plenty of the long green, and then all of a sudden she stopped paying. How I know this is, I was sort of a fixer for Alton, you know what I mean?"

"I know what you mean," Shigata said. "Go on."

"So Alton had the hots for her, and so he said he'd take it out in play, only she had to stop gambling. And if she wouldn't stop gambling, then she had to come up with the cash some way if she had to do it on her back. So she did. But she couldn't get out real regular at first, said her old man—Are you *really* a fed? You ain't pulling my leg?"

"I'm really a fed."

"Married to a hooker. Don't that beat all."

Shigata agreed that beat all.

"Okay, so she was back in the life again and she liked it a lot more than she did when she was a kid. She'd growed up, so to speak. And she said her old man was a real three-dimensional nerd. You don't look like no nerd to me. You look classy. I wisht I was classy."

"But she said I was a nerd. Go on and tell me. I'm not going to get mad at you. This is stuff I need to know."

"Yeah. She said you was a nerd. Because you didn't like to party. And she liked to party. So Alton, he told her to move out, move to the Island and he'd see to it she got to party. So she did. And he took her to Houston a lot. The place she moved into, I mean, it was a dump, it was as bad as this place of mine. But she wasn't there much, you know what I mean?"

"I know what you mean. So it was Alton running her."

"Yeah."

"So where's Alton?" Shigata asked patiently.

"What do you need to know that for?"

"I told you what for. Because I need to know, that's what for."

"Well, okay, but I sure don't see why. I mean, he sure as hell didn't knock off Wendy or that other dame you said. At least not unless it was done a while back."

"How come you're so sure?" Quinn asked resignedly.

"Because Alton, he had a stroke three weeks ago and they took him over to UTMB and he died. That's how come."

twelve

"**A**L?"

"Yeah?"

"Don't do it again."

Stopped at a red light on Seawall Boulevard, Quinn glanced over at Shigata. "Play tough cop, you mean? I don't do it so good, do I?"

"You don't know when to bluster and when not to. So it doesn't work. You nearly lost that witness for us. Don't do it again."

"Yassuh, massuh . . . I do the dumb cop real good, though, don't I?"

Shigata closed his eyes, trying without much success not to chuckle.

Quinn began to laugh. "You should've seen the look on your face when I started crunching those carrots! Man, I had to *work* to chew that loud!"

"Why in the world did you want to do it?"

Quinn chuckled again. "I knew you needed to see that evidence and you needed another look at the crime scene when you weren't so emotionally wound up as you were last night. But if you'd just gone over there like a nice little gentleman—you Bureau boys being the notorious gentlemen you are—and asked, they'd have said no. Quite properly, you being their main suspect. So I figured I'd get 'em so grossed out they'd do *anything* to get rid of me." He sobered. "Thing is, they know me. Both of them. They know how I work and they know I get good results. But they also know any time they tell me no I'll drive 'em crazy. And I'll do it in public."

"It looks so damned unprofessional, though."

"Oh well. My department needs somebody real polished to balance against me." He glanced at Shigata. "You know, somebody like a good chief, maybe."

"Your department doesn't need a chief who's liable to be in jail for murder before next week's out."

"You won't be in jail. *Shim-pai-nai.*"

"I wish you'd quit talking Japanese to me. It makes me feel inferior when I don't know what you mean."

"Okay. What was that address for Andrea?"

"It's not in Galveston."

"I *know* it's not in Galveston, that's why I'm on Broadway headed for the causeway. But what town *is* it in?"

"Oh. Bayport. It's—Hold on while I get my notebook out. All right, it's seven thirty-one Prune Street. Ye gods and little fishes. Who'd want to live on Prune Street?"

"Andrea Collins. I hope. That address is over thirteen years old."

It was a small house with white asbestos siding now mildewed to a dismal grey. The yard had been mowed, but not recently, and the morning newspaper in its plastic wrapper still lay in the driveway. A small tabby cat sitting on the front porch stood up at their arrival, eyed them briefly, and turned to skitter under the house.

Friday's mail hadn't been taken out of the mailbox. And the name on the mailbox said A. Collins.

The house was quiet.

"She still lives here, apparently," Shigata said. "But it looks like she's gone somewhere. Could be—"

"Yeah. Could be she's gone to the morgue."

"I'll get the neighbors on the left."

"Right. I'll go on the other side."

The neighbors on the left consisted, at the moment, of one boy who claimed to be sixteen but was at least a foot taller than Shigata. "You must be a good basketball player," Shigata commented.

With indignation shining on his dark brown face, the boy retorted, "Basketball! Mr. Shigata, I play an oboe!"

"You play what?"

"An oboe! You know what an oboe sounds like?"

"Yes. Beautiful. What I—"

"Want me to show you?"

"No, I—"

"It's right here, it won't take a minute."

"I don't *have* a spare minute right now."

"Chinks don't like oboes?"

"I'm not Chinese! I'm Nisei—Japanese American. And I love oboes. Give a concert and I'll come. But right now I need to ask you some questions. It's very important and I don't have time to spare. Believe me, if I had time I'd love to hear you. I used to play an oboe when I was a kid. But the questions now."

"You used to play an oboe?"

"Yeah, I played one when I was a kid. Questions now."

"Yeah. Okay." The boy composed his long legs on a too-small chintz-covered couch and looked expectant.

"Could I have your name, to start with?"

"Douglas Booker. What's all this about, anyway?"

"It's hard to say yet. I need to talk to Andrea Collins. Does she still live next door to you?"

"Miz Collins? Oh yeah. She's too mean to move away. We rent this house from her, and she won't paint it. It sure does need it."

"Yeah, I hear you. Landladies can be like that. But what I—"

"Well, she says she can't afford to. What I'm talking about is the homework. She pours it on. She's the meanest durn teacher in the whole school—six pages of homework, and it's *Friday!*"

"Teacher? What does she teach?" The body from his backyard hadn't looked like a teacher. So maybe Andrea Collins was missing for some other reason. Maybe that wasn't her in the morgue.

"Math. You know, algebra and trig. And what's really rotten is, she looks like a doll—what I mean, a real doll, one you could take home in your pocket, and this friend of mine, Billy, says he's heard when she was just a kid she used to be a stripper, but then she went to college and— What's so funny?"

"It's not funny." Shigata composed himself, trying not to think of a stripper teaching trig. "It's not funny at all. But I need to see a copy of your school yearbook. You got one?"

"Well, yeah, but why—?"

"Will you get it for me?"

"Well, it's upstairs in my bedroom. You don't mind waiting?"

"No, I don't mind waiting."

Douglas climbed the stairs, his head at one point nearly brushing the ceiling of the overhead landing, and returned a moment later with a book colorfully blazoned with a picture of a huge barracuda. "Bayport 'Cudas," he said proudly. "That's another thing I do, besides play the oboe. I'm on the annual staff. Wasn't this a good cover?"

"Yeah, real eyecatching," Shigata agreed. "Can you find a picture of Miss Collins for me?"

"Yeah, sure, just a minute. Here she is."

There was no possible doubt. Their expensive-looking corpse—their possible callgirl—was a high-school mathematics teacher.

"Was she at school yesterday?"

"Yeah, why?"

"Did you see her after you got home yesterday, out in the yard or anything?"

"Uh-uh. She didn't go home. She told me—I got seventh period with her—she told me she was gonna be late getting home and would I feed her cat. So I did. But she never lets that cat stay out overnight, and I noticed when I got home from my date her car wasn't in the driveway and the cat was still out. And when I got up this morning it was still the same way. Mr. Shigata, do you think she's a spy or something? I mean, the FBI doesn't usually—"

"No, she's not a spy. This isn't Bureau business. I'm just sort of helping out the local police. We think something might have happened to her. How did you get in her house to get the catfood?"

"I don't have to get in the house. I feed her cat lots

when she's gone, and so I keep catfood over here. But usually if she's going to be gone overnight she gives me the keys so I can let the cat in. What do you think might have happened?"

"I'd rather not guess just yet. I need to do some more checking."

"Has it got anything to do with her sister?"

"Her sister?" Wendy was her sister. "What do you know about her sister?"

"Oh, you didn't know that? Well, this week, I think it was Wednesday, her sister came over to visit her after school and there was some kind of great big row. I don't know what all happened, but I know there was a lot of commotion."

"Tell me about it."

"All I know is, her sister come over in this red car and then somebody else come driving up real fast and Miz Collins and her sister took off in Miz Collins's car and the other car took off after them and that's all I know. Except Miz Collins came back later and her sister got in her car and drove off."

Wednesday. The day Wendy probably died. "What did the other car look like, the one that was chasing Miss Collins and her sister?"

"Gee, I dunno. It was gray. Like Miz Collins's car, only bigger. And shaped different."

"Gray? That's all you know on either one? No make or model or anything?"

"Well, I don't pay much attention to cars." Douglas fondled his oboe, glanced at the yearbook. "I got other things on my mind."

Ten thousand high-school boys know every car on the

road, Shigata thought. I get one that plays the oboe. "What did the driver look like?"

"Of the gray car? I never did see that driver."

"And you said Miss Collins's sister was driving a red car?" Wendy's car was a yellow Mustang.

"A foxy-looking red car. She's pretty, she looked a lot like Miz Collins. You know, blonde and built."

"Blonde?" Wendy had lived and died a brunette. That, they were sure of.

"Yeah, blonde. She was taller than Miz Collins."

"Would you recognize her if you saw her again?"

"Oh, yeah. Her I'd recognize. Her car I wouldn't but I would her."

Shigata had meant a thousand times to take Wendy's picture out of his billfold; maybe it was fortunate he hadn't. "Is this Miss Collins's sister?"

Douglas looked at the photo. "Uh-uh. She was pretty. But not that pretty. That lady in the picture, she's a real fox. Miz Collins's sister, she—Well, I don't know, she might be foxy, too, except—"

"Except what?"

"Except she looked scared. Mister Shigata, I *never* seen a lady look so scared before. Like the devil was riding on her coattails."

"Our callgirl was a math teacher," Quinn said.

"So I found out. You get any kind of a description of those cars?"

"Those which cars?"

"Wednesday. Her sister and somebody chasing her sister."

"Wendy, you mean, somebody chasing Wendy? On *Wednesday?* Great! No, nobody told me—"

"Not Wendy," Shigata interrupted. "Seems she had another sister. A blonde. You didn't get any of that?"

Quinn sighed. "Brother, I got a retired mail carrier who moved here from Iowa three weeks ago and has been too busy planting a fall garden to meet his neighbors. I got two Mormon missionaries and one of them has been here six weeks and one of them has been here four days, and all either one of them can tell me is the lady living in this house told them she had six copies of the Book of Mormon already and go practice on somebody else. I got a Mrs. Jenkins who says Miss Collins is probably no better than she should be even if she is a teacher. But she also says she spent the last week with her daughter who just had a baby, and she's not been home an hour, and she doesn't know what Miss Collins did this week and cares less. Want me to go on?"

"The rest about the same?"

"Those were the good ones."

"No, I don't want you to go on. Al, tell me something. You're the only detective on your department, right?"

"Right."

"So what happens if something else goes down while you're spending all your time with me?"

"Danged if I know. I guess uniform division works it."

"But—"

"Told you we need a chief. Gotta get somebody to ride herd on me."

"Quinn."

"Shigata, we're gonna *get* a chief one of these days. Can you blame me for trying to get my candidate elected?"

"Buddy, your candidate's not running."

thirteen

SHE SAW HIM WALKING ON THE BEACH.

Daddy.

It had to be Daddy. The right hair, the right color of skin, the way he walked, the way he held his head. She was too far away to see his face, but—

But Daddy didn't wear cowboy boots. And Daddy didn't wear jeans, except on weekends.

So why was he walking on the beach in jeans and cowboy boots to look for her?

And he was looking for her. She was sure of that because he was looking at every girl on the beach who was anything like her size and coloring, looking hard, looking like—like he was almost not sure he would recognize her.

And that was funny too.

But if she didn't want him to find her she'd better get away from the beach.

Andrea should be home by now, no matter where she'd gone.

Melissa's hands clutched the steering wheel tightly; she almost expected Sam's car to career around the corner again, the way it had done on Wednesday, before—At the thought of that she began to shake almost uncontrollably.

But no, he wasn't there and he wasn't coming there.

He wasn't there, she reassured herself again.

But neither was Andrea.

Where could she *be?* Unwillingly, Melissa's mind slipped back. She'd fled Wendy's house, leaving Sam and Wendy fighting; she'd left Wendy to die but she'd had no way of knowing that, she'd thought Sam wouldn't hurt Wendy. He'd always liked Wendy. He said Wendy had the spunk to fight back. ·

Melissa wasn't allowed to fight back.

So she left Sam and Wendy fighting and she ran away, taking Wendy's address book, because if Wendy didn't have Gail (and all that money she'd given Wendy to look after Gail, how long had it been that Wendy didn't have Gail?) maybe she'd written it down in her address book. Maybe she'd written something down to tell where Gail was.

She'd left the address book at Andrea's house by accident on Wednesday; she and Andrea had been looking through it and somehow it hadn't gotten back into her purse. She didn't have it anymore.

And she didn't have the jewelry box Wendy gave her only three months ago, the jewelry box with all her pictures of Gail, because when she went back to get it Sam got it.

Or somebody got it.

It must be Sam, nobody else would want it, but it couldn't be Sam because he would have found her, as well as the jewelry box, and that person didn't find her, but it must be Sam because who else would have taken the jewelry box and nothing else?

So now he'd have the pictures. And now he'd know. Now he'd know the child was alive, now he'd know the child was a girl, now he'd know—

Oh no. Oh no. She'd forgotten *that* picture.

All the other pictures were Gail alone, Gail with Wendy, one very old one of Gail with Melissa. But there was that one picture, Gail with—Gail with Wendy's husband. So Sam would know that. Sam would know. And Sam hated Asians. Hated them. He'd enjoyed killing that boy, she knew that, and now he'd know—

Melissa was afraid to go back to Andrea's house after Sam was arrested, after Andrea called the police to report he was causing a public disturbance. Because she knew Sam would get out of jail fast. With his money, he wouldn't stay in jail long. So she went back to Andrea's just long enough to get her car, and she hurried home while Sam was still in jail and got some clothes. But Sam must have gotten out of jail while she was there because—

That still didn't make sense.

But she didn't dare go from there to Wendy's because Sam would look for her at Wendy's. But after he had had time to look for her, then she would go to Wendy's. Not to Andrea's. Not to Andrea's because Andrea would ask too many questions. And Sam might go to Andrea's house anyway, whether he was hunting Melissa or not.

Andrea had laughed and laughed after she called the police. Melissa couldn't make her understand. And it was too late now.

In one of the suitcases she'd found a forgotten book of

traveler's checks, left over from the last time they went to Vegas. That helped; she went to Houston and hid in a motel.

But they didn't add up to very much money, and she had to have gasoline, food. So, finally, figuring Sam had by now had time to look for her at Wendy's and give up on that location, she'd tried to go back there. And that was when she found Wendy, and realized Sam had killed her.

She got back out of that house just in time, just before those other two men, one of them a policeman, she guessed, and the other that must be Wendy's husband, went into the house. She sat in her car up the street and watched until she knew the body was gone. She waited a little longer, and she saw them take Wendy's husband out on a stretcher. It had to be Wendy's husband out on a stretcher. It had to be Wendy's husband, with those eyes, but he looked so much like Sam it was terrifying, although she knew he wasn't Sam because she'd seen Sam on the beach while that man was in the house.

Hoping Sam was still on the beach, she hurried home— back to Sam's house to get clothes. Hurried fast, so she could get there and leave before Sam got home. And then she went to Andrea's house, because that was the only place left to go.

Andrea would ask a lot of questions, she knew. Andrea would fuss. But Andrea would take her in even if it was midnight or later.

That was what she had told herself. And maybe it was true, but Andrea wasn't there and she didn't know how to break in, even into Andrea's house.

Melissa slept in the car for a while, before she remembered the key Wendy gave her six months ago, gave her for a joke. But if she was right, if that was Wendy's husband they'd taken to the hospital, that would be a safe place. For one night.

She went to Wendy's husband's house. And she slept there.

Slept there in what must be Wendy's husband's bed, although she'd found the bedroom that had to be Gail's bedroom, found it and sat in it and wept because Gail wasn't there, although she didn't have any idea what she would have done if Gail had been there.

She didn't sleep in Gail's bed because she felt dirty, unclean, a kind of unclean soap and water won't take off, and she didn't want that on Gail's bed.

But at least she slept. For a while, before she got up and went to the front porch and got Wendy's husband's newspaper and saw that Gail was missing. Really missing, and nobody knew where she was.

And she went off so fast she left that little black thing Sam used to hit her with. She'd taken it, when she ran away, so that she'd have at least a little protection, because she was scared of guns even though she knew where Sam kept his guns.

And besides that she'd left the bottle of bourbon she'd taken out of Wendy's house.

The bourbon wasn't important. But the little black thing was, because it was the only weapon she had. But she was afraid to go back looking for it, because Wendy's husband might not still be in the hospital.

She felt like she ought to be looking for Gail, and she went and walked up and down the beach because when she was a kid she went to the beach when she was scared and lonesome and Gail might be like her. But then she wasn't even sure she would recognize Gail if she did see her.

So she went back to Andrea's house a couple of times, but Andrea still wasn't there.

Andrea—

Andrea was dead.

The thought slid unbidden into her mind. Andrea was dead. Andrea had to be dead. Sam had killed her too; that was the only answer.

Melissa began again to cry. And she didn't know whether she was crying for Wendy and Andrea, or because she no longer had anywhere to go. Not anywhere at all.

Ellen Watson looked somewhat more like a high-school principal than Andrea Collins had looked like a teacher. She was tall, a little overweight but not really fat. An imposing woman, with a crisp businesslike voice. You'd think twice before crossing her. She had neat gray hair, and at nine o'clock Saturday night she was wearing tailored gray gabardine slacks, a white blouse, and a gray tweed jacket.

She did not go girlish in the morgue. She looked at the body carefully, with no more sign of emotion than blinking eyelids, twitching nostrils, and said, "Yes, that's Andrea. How terrible! Does anyone know yet who did it?"

"No, ma'am, not yet," Quinn answered.

He was not putting on any kind of an act with her, Shigata noticed, and was not surprised when she said, "Well, Albert, I was afraid someday her past would catch up with her."

"What past was that, Mrs. Watson?"

"You wouldn't remember her, of course, she was probably eight years or so behind you. But she was terribly wild as a young girl. In fact, she dropped out of high school at seventeen to become a prostitute." Mrs. Watson's voice carried no particular inflection; she was merely stating a fact. "Eventually she realized that it was not the major course she wanted her life to take. She came to me and asked me to help her make new plans. She had quite a good mind, and I was happy to work with her. I was so delighted for her when she was finally able to get her degree. But occasionally it would happen that she would—rather embarrassingly—meet one of her former casual customers. She really should have left the area. But she told me she couldn't. She was quite fond of the beach, of course—you've probably noticed that just from looking at the body. I pointed out to her she could sun elsewhere if she insisted on risking skin cancer, and she told me that wasn't it—the problem was her sister. She said her sister needed her badly."

"Which sister was that, Mrs. Watson?" Quinn asked.

"I'm not sure of that. But she seemed rather distraught the last couple of days, quite unlike her normal manner, and I asked her if there was any problem. She told me her sister might be in serious trouble and she was unsure what to do to help. I suggested she take a couple of days off to work on the problem, that I could get a substitute for her. But of course you know good mathematics teachers are very scarce, and she was quite conscientious. It will be difficult to replace her, poor girl. We'll miss her, even the students. They grumbled about her but I think secretly most of them were delighted to have the discipline."

"Mrs. Watson, did she ever use another name?"

"Why, yes. She went by the name of Andrea Blair all

the way through high school and on through her—through the more unsavory part of her life. But Collins was her real name, and she resumed it when she started working on her GED, before trying to get into college."

"Blair?" Shigata asked sharply. The stepsister listed on Wendy's arrest record was named Blair. Melissa Blair.

"Yes. It was all rather complicated." They were leaving the morgue, going back out into the windy autumn night. "You see, she was the middle of three girls. She had an older half sister, Wendy Collins, whose mother had died in childbirth. The father remarried quite early, and then when Andrea was only a few months old, Mr. Collins was killed in an accident. Mrs. Collins later remarried, to a Mr. Blair, and they had a daughter, Melissa. Thus, of course, Andrea was half sister to both Wendy and Melissa, but Wendy and Melissa were no more than stepsisters although of course the girls were always treated as sisters. Not well treated, I might add. If you wonder how I know all this, well, I taught all three girls, and in addition Andrea lived with me for several months when she was first trying to get into college."

"She still doesn't look like a math teacher to me," Quinn said.

"Well—" Mrs. Watson looked oddly embarrassed. "I'm afraid that Andrea never did rid herself of the habit of—ah—having rich boyfriends. And accepting expensive presents from them. Quite discreetly, of course, and only one man at a time—she tended toward rather long-term relationships. But she never could understand it was in any way either wrong or unsafe. Why, even her voice changed when she was around what she saw as potential prey—if you'll pardon that way of putting it. I saw her that way once, at a party. With the children she was all business, but around a rich man, in a party situation, her voice became a throaty purr. It was quite astonishing. And, of course, the school board cannot regulate the teachers' behavior, as long as they do their work adequately. Which Andrea did. As I said, she was quite discreet. And there is *such* a shortage of mathematics teachers."

"Did she have a current boyfriend?" Shigata asked.

"She didn't talk to me about them—she knew I disapproved. But I think she did. For several months she'd been looking even better groomed than usual. And I overheard the conclusion of a conversation she was having with one of the other teachers in the lounge one day. I had the feeling she'd picked this one out of some spirit of revenge, to get even, as she put it, for something this man had done in the past. But I really didn't hear any more than that, and I don't think I noticed who she was talking with."

They got the names of Andrea's friends.

They did not get a description of Andrea's car; Mrs. Watson said she had recently bought a new one. "Not *new* new," she explained, "but new to Andrea."

"Mrs. Watson, I think you've done more to help us out than anyone else we've talked with in the last two days," Quinn said. "Just one thing more. Do you have anything listing her next of kin? We very much need to find someone to notify."

"I'm sorry, Albert, but that is in the superintendent's office. I'll be happy to attempt to locate him for you."

"I wish you would do that. I'll give you my home telephone number. Will you call me as soon as you reach him?"

"Certainly." She seemed to hesitate. "Albert. Did—did

anyone ever find out any more about what happened to Mark?''

"No, ma'am. We still don't know any more. And probably never will.''

"I'm very sorry. He was a fine lad.'' She turned then, to walk toward her car.

"She was my English teacher,'' Quinn said. "All four years. Bless her heart, I guess I should say she *tried* to teach me English.'' He fumbled in his pocket for car keys. "Well. That gives us another reason to find Melissa Blair.''

"Next of kin,'' Shigata agreed. "And hope to hell she's not dead too.''

The address they had for Melissa Blair was about as no good as an address could get. A three-block area surrounding it had been razed and replaced by a sprawl of apartment buildings on streets relaid and renamed.

"Any other ideas?'' Quinn asked, resting his hands on the steering wheel.

"Yes. We go to Galveston. We were looking for information on Andrea Collins. Now we go back and look for information on Andrea Blair.''

"They searched her prints, from the corpse. If she'd been there they would have found her no matter what name she was using.''

"So I'm stubborn. Galveston.''

They went back to Galveston.

She'd been arrested three times. Her fingerprints were wide whorls; they had not been fully rolled on one of the three arrests. And there they sat in a drawer marked "unclassifiable.''

But there was no next of kin except Melissa Blair and

Wendy Collins. And the address for Melissa Blair was the one they'd already checked.

"I don't know about you," Quinn said, "but I'm pooped."

"I don't feel like I ought to be stopping to rest when—"

"When Gail is still missing. You know she's looking after herself; we've had enough people see her for you to know that. Anyway, what good'll you do her dead?"

"Why would I be dead?"

"If I get much tireder I'm perfectly likely to cream this car. And don't offer to drive because you're just as tired as I am."

Neither one of them noticed the gray Mercedes parked near Shigata's driveway, Quinn because he was unfamiliar with the neighborhood and didn't know it wasn't always there, Shigata because he was just too tired to see it.

Or maybe he did see it. Maybe he saw it but just didn't notice it, not until after Quinn drove away and Shigata, walking toward his front door, felt a gun in his ribs. He tried to turn and someone grabbed him, and he tried to turn the other way and somebody else grabbed him, and he tried belatedly to draw and felt his pistol leaving his holster as he slapped for it.

fourteen

HE HAD A BEWILDERING SENSATION OF DIS-
orientation; they turned him around several times and it
was dark, the street light was out—how had it gotten
out?—and hands were on him and he didn't know how
many. "Where is she?" a hoarse voice demanded almost
in his ear.

"Who?" All his confusion poured into the one word.

"You're in no situation to play games, bastard, and I
ain't gonna dirty my fists on you. I'll ask it one more time.
Where is she?"

"I don't know—"

He didn't even know who they were asking about. But
they didn't let him finish saying it. Somebody crammed
something in his mouth, a handkerchief he thought, and
tied it tight around the back of his head. They half
marched, half dragged him around the house into what
was left of the unused garage he'd been tearing down.
They pulled his unbuttoned jacket off; it caught on the
strap of his watch and took it off too. They yanked his shirt

off, roughly, tearing buttons, and they tore his undershirt off him from the back, not allowing it to go off over his head.

Raw fear was boiling up inside him, fear mixed with a dazed sensation of utter disbelief. Things like this don't happen. Not really. Only in movies, bad movies at that, the kind he didn't go to see.

They tied his arms to an overhanging bicycle rack. Too high. His heels couldn't reach the ground. His toes could, barely, but the position made him fight for breath.

He didn't know what they hit him with, whether it was a whip or a belt. Only that it hurt. Worse than it should have, he thought; it shouldn't be bad until it had gone on a while. But it started out bad.

Maybe he would have yelled, but the gag caught whatever sound he was going to make.

They went on hitting him, again and again and again and he didn't want to count but he couldn't stop counting—eight, nine, ten—and the pain went on building and it couldn't get any worse—seventeen, eighteen, nineteen, and it went on getting worse and worse when it couldn't get any worse, his body wouldn't hold any more but it went on—thirty, thirty-one, wouldn't it ever stop—

Even with the gag he was getting louder. He wondered where his pride was, to let them know—he guessed he didn't have any pride left right now.

The whip—he guessed it was a whip—stopped on sixty-three.

The pain didn't.

Somebody untied the gag.

He tried to hold back the sounds. He couldn't. He was crying and he couldn't stop crying and he'd lost control of his bladder and bowels and he couldn't stop crying and if they hit him again he was going to die.

Only, of course, he wasn't going to die.

No such luck.

"Where is she, gook? The girl? Where is she?"

The girl. Gail. They meant Gail.

They wanted Gail. Why? And why did they think he knew where she was?

"I know that's just a smokescreen, her run away like the papers said. You've got her hid. Where is she?"

The man's mask had slipped or else he'd taken it off or else he hadn't been wearing one. They weren't all wearing masks. Shigata stared at him, puzzled, startled. It was like looking into a distorted mirror. The man was almost exactly his size, and his facial features were similar, except that he was a round-eye.

"Answer me, you flat-faced bastard."

"I don't know where she is. And if I knew I wouldn't tell you."

He hoped that was true. He was afraid by now he'd sell his soul to keep them from hitting him again.

His soul maybe.

But not his child.

Not Gail.

The man's face was wildly distorted with rage. "You son-of-a-bitching Jap bastard, I'll break you in two!"

"You can do that. But you can't make me sell my daughter. I don't know where she is. I wish I did know. But I'll never tell you." Big words. Big words when tears were still running down his face, when he could feel something even more humiliating wet in his trousers.

"*Your* daughter—you Goddamn slant-eyed son-of-a-bitch—'' The man was raging. "She ain't no gook—" The man was incoherent. Shigata saw him blindly reaching for—Yes, it was a whip. A big one. He wasn't sure he'd ever seen a whip before.

Whips cut. The layer of skin over muscle is tough but not that tough. The layer of muscle over bone is thin along the back. God. No. Please. Not any more.

He managed not to say that aloud. They'd have enjoyed hearing it.

"The gag, Sam," somebody said fast. "The neighbors—"

They jammed the gag back into his mouth. It was cold now from being away from his mouth, and slimy, and he retched uncontrollably. They released it just long enough to keep him from choking to death, and then tightened it again.

It started again.

It was worse than it was before and he thought in dazed confusion, "But I'm a small man. My body isn't big enough to hold this much."

But you never know. You never know.

After a while he didn't even want to scream anymore. He wanted them to stop hitting him and go away so he could sleep. But that was dangerous, he thought. That was the wrong thing to want. That was too close to wanting to die. And he couldn't die, not die and leave Gail alone.

"Any more now'll kill him, Sam. Then he sure won't tell you. Anyway, I got to—"

"Yeah, yeah, I know. It's almost eleven. But we'll be back, you slope-headed son of a bitch. We'll be back. And next time you'll have the right answer."

They must have untied him. He didn't know when they did that, but he was lying on the ground.

He managed to work the gag off.

His keys were still in his pants pocket. So was the card with Quinn's home phone number. He found his gun on the ground and put it back into his holster without checking to see if it was loaded.

He didn't remember going inside, or picking up the phone, but he must have, because he was sitting on the couch holding the phone in his hand staring at it hazily, hearing it ring at the other end. He hoped he'd dialed the right number. He couldn't remember dialing.

A woman answered.

"Al," he said.

"Al is asleep. Very tired."

"Al," he said again. "Please. Please."

"Al is *very* tired."

"Please. Al."

A rustling sound. A thump. More rustling.

"Quinn." A sleepy voice. A rough voice. Al is very tired. Mark is very tired.

"Al."

"Yeah. Shigata. That you?"

"Yes. Please—Al—"

"Are you okay?" The voice had snapped to alertness.

"No. Help—I—" Why couldn't he talk? Why wouldn't his teeth stop chattering? He tried again. "Al—"

"I'm on my way."

"Yeah." He dropped the phone in the general vicinity of the switchhook and collapsed across the couch. It wasn't the pain that woke him. It was the sound of himself crying.

"Be still," Quinn told him. "I'm trying to wash the blood off. Do you want me to call an ambulance?"

"No." He set his teeth to try to keep quiet. It wasn't easy.

"I didn't think so. That's why I didn't call one. I'm sorry—I'm trying not to hurt you."

"You can't—not—hurt—Oh, God, I'm—trying—"

"I know you're trying, Mark. It's okay. Can you manage to tell me about it, do you think?"

"Not now—*unh*—" He concentrated on breathing. Maybe if he concentrated hard on breathing—

He couldn't concentrate hard enough on breathing to block out the pain. But he managed to stay fairly quiet for Al's sake. His pride wasn't sufficient to keep him quiet while they were doing it, but he didn't want to hurt Al by making a lot of noise when Al was trying to help him.

It must have been ten minutes before Al said, "Mark, buddy, that's all I can do. You need a doctor."

They hadn't been a pleasant ten minutes.

He went on concentrating on breathing. Al didn't say anything. Al didn't touch him. Al just waited.

It was another couple of minutes before he was able to get his breath enough to start talking. "They were KKK, some of them anyway. I recognized a few of them but I don't remember well enough to tie names to faces. I'll find that out later. But there was something else—something about Gail. They wanted me to tell them where Gail was. And—there was one—" He described Sam. "And he—it was like he went crazy, I mean crazier than he was already, I mean really crazy, when I told him I wouldn't sell him my daughter."

•

"Mark. Gail has a natural mother alive. We know that now. Could be she has a natural father alive too."

"Yeah. I thought of that."

"He must have just now found out about her. And he wants her."

"He won't get her. I'd kill him first. I—Al. I love that kid. You know I do. But I think—I think if, if I had to, if it was the only way I could keep him from getting her, I'd kill *her* before I'd let him have her. Al. What would her life be *like*—"

"You wouldn't do that."

"No. You're right. Of course I wouldn't. But I'd kill him. I will kill him, if it looks like—"

"I'd help. If it came to that."

"Would you?"

"Or maybe I'd just kill him for you."

"Would you?"

"Mark, you're feeling what it feels like to live in your skin right now, and I'd say it ain't no fun. Me, I'm looking at it from the outside, and it don't look like fun from where I sit. Let that blackhearted bastard get ahold of a girl child? Yes, I'll kill him if I have to." He backed off a little. "Shigata, you need to go to the hospital."

"I'm not going to the hospital."

"Well, you're damn sure not staying here."

"But—"

"Come on over to my house. I'll call Nguyen and let her know you're coming. She'll double the kids up or something and make a place for you to sleep."

"Al, I—"

"Don't argue. I need more sleep tonight even if you

don't and I ain't going to get it if I have to keep running over here."

"Al—" He didn't know whether he was laughing or crying.

"Quit arguing. Get a fast shower. You stink. I'll find you some clothes. And have you got any whiskey? A stiff drink here, another one at my house, and you ought to sleep—"

"I don't have any whiskey."

"Yes, you do, here it is."

He was too sleepy to wonder where it came from. He just drank out of the glass Al gave him.

He blinked in the light. He'd fallen asleep in the car.

Nguyen was short, dumpy, and pregnant. Quinn patted her protuberance and told Shigata, "This'll make eleven."

"Twelve," she said quickly.

"Yeah," he agreed, "twelve. But I—" He stopped and they looked at each other, joined by a tangible grief that excluded Shigata along with the rest of the world.

Then Quinn stepped back a little, to include him again. "Well! Where is our guest going to sleep?"

"Oh! It was ver' easy. Eddie and Stevie and Johnnie are on the boat with Hoa. Tomorrow they are going fishing. So I just sent the little boys back to their own room and our guest have room all alone." She smiled.

Quinn smiled too. "This way."

"Thank you," Shigata told her, and she smiled again, brilliantly, and for a moment was almost pretty.

"You need another drink?" Quinn asked.

"I'm okay."

"I think we've got some codeine."

"I'm okay. You don't look old enough to have that many kids."

"Me? I'm forty-eight. How old did you think I was?"

"Then you're older than I am. I thought you were about thirty or thirty-five."

Al Quinn's laughter was a low rumble. "All us round-eyes look alike. It's clean living does it, and let me tell you, brother, when you got this many kids, you ain't got the time *or* the money to do anything *but* live clean. You sure you don't need anything?"

"Just sleep. I'm okay."

"I'll get the light. . . . Shigata?"

"Yeah?"

Quinn had paused in the darkness, his hand still on the light switch. Then he walked back across the room, and Quinn heard springs creaking as he sat down on the opposite bed. "Buddy, there's something wrong with you."

"Yeah, I just got the crap beat out of me, that's what's wrong with me."

"I don't mean that. Something else. Listen. I got to tell you this and I—it's not what I usually talk about. I mean I don't like to—"

He started over. "I married Nguyen in Nam. She was already pregnant and I—we don't talk about it, neither one of us, but Johnnie, my oldest, he's twenty, he—he might not be mine. You know? We just don't know. Like I said, we don't talk about it. He don't know. He never will know. But I was scared she'd—maybe get hurt, there was fighting everywhere and car bombs and stuff, so I got her on a plane and sent her to my mom. And—and I was captured, a week later. Eight months. Eight months. Brother, I know what it is to hurt, and hurt, and hurt, and hurt, and want to sleep to get out of it because that's the only way out. Only then, the hurting wakes you up and you want to die because that's the only way to stay asleep— I *know.* You're saying you'll be okay. Well, you will. You're saying it but you don't know it. Me, I do know it. Believe it or not, you'll be okay. That way. But—"

"But what?"

"Don't hate, Shigata. Don't hate. Don't let them make you hate. When you hate, it don't hurt who you hate. It just hurts you. The guys kept talking about the slant-eyes. The gooks. The rice-eaters. Hate. Hate. Hate. But—I'd married Nguyen and she'd gone to a foreign land where she didn't know anybody and didn't speak the language and she was waiting for me. For me. And there was the baby coming. And I could hate or I could not hate. And— I thought—it wasn't because they were slant-eyes that they were hurting me. It was because of the way they were taught. And I could teach my kids. I *would* teach my kids, whether I meant to or not, because they'd be there, they'd see, they'd hear. So I could teach my kids to hate the shape of their eyes, hate their—their heritage. Or I could teach them to hate me. If I wanted to. Or maybe even if I didn't want to, if I went at things all wrong. Or I could learn to like fish sauce and speak Vietnamese and let them know their mama's world is okay too."

"So you learned to speak Vietnamese and like fish sauce."

"Well, I still don't like fish sauce. The damn stuff stinks. You ever smelled it being made? No, of course you haven't. Damn, it stinks. But my kids—they wear Levis and cowboy boots and they have slant eyes. They eat hamburgers and hot dogs and they eat rice and fish sauce. They talk Vietnamese with Uncle Hoa on the shrimp boat, and they play video games at Seven-Eleven if they mow lawns to get the quarters, because I damn sure won't give them quarters to feed the idiot box. Shigata, I'm not saying don't do what you have to do. I've killed. I killed to get out of that—place. I don't know how many people I've killed. But I killed to stay alive. I killed without hating. You. Tell me. Why wouldn't they let you be Japanese?"

"Because of when I was born. February 1942. I—my aunt, my dad's favorite sister, had shot herself. On Pearl Harbor Day. In the college dorm. With a rifle—she was on the intercollegiate rifle team, so she had the key to the ammunition locker and all, and she just—couldn't—" He took a deep breath. "And my dad—it was weeks before they'd let him enlist. He couldn't even get into the recruiting station without somebody jumping him. And—and after the war, he wouldn't associate even with his own family, except this one brother, Henry. Henry had a son—my cousin—he was named Henry too, only—well, Henry married an Anglo, and after he died—"

"Which Henry married an Anglo? Your uncle or your cousin?"

"My uncle. He died when I was about twelve or so. And then I never did see my cousin again after that. I don't know where they went. I think his mother took him away somewhere."

"Your uncle as nutty as your dad?"

In the darkness, Shigata grimaced. "Worse," he said briefly.

"Your mom?"

"She's okay. She went to live with her parents after my dad died. They live in California. They're named Omori."

"Yeah? You got any Omori cousins?"

"About a million, I think. But I don't know any of them."

"Why not?"

"Because my dad wouldn't let us visit them. After he died, I visited a few times. But I was in college then and I—I always felt like an alien there. I mean—they were Americans but they were—were in touch with Japan. But my dad—he—he wanted to get some kind of surgery on my eyes, even, so they wouldn't look—but my mom drew the line at that, she was afraid it would affect my vision, and they had a really big fight over it and that's the only fight my dad ever lost. But he wouldn't even let me *say* I was Japanese. Not even Nisei. We were Americans. Americans. Americans. I had to look in the dictionary to find out how to pronounce Nisei. You ever memorize the Constitution?"

"The *whole* Constitution?" Quinn asked incredulously. "No. The Preamble, in the seventh grade, only I didn't. We the people—that's all I remember."

"The whole Constitution, right through the Bill of Rights. My dad made me."

"Okay. But—"

"We were the WASPest Japs you ever saw, Al."

Quinn laughed again, very softly. "Okay. But don't hate. Round-eyes or slant-eyes. Japanese WASPs or the KKK. Hate what they do if you need to. Kill if you need to. I've done it and I'll do it again if I have to. But don't hate. And—Mark."

"Yeah?"

"Brother, sometime when you get a chance, learn to be Japanese."

The door closed softly behind him.

Late, late in the night Mark Shigata half woke to the sound of a muffled moan in the room next to him. He'd hurt too much lately, physically and emotionally, to tune that sound out; he was fully awake instantly.

Then he heard the sound again, and this time he knew it for what it was.

The stocky, ruddy, rednecked farmer who somewhat incongruously wore a gun and badge, who even more incongruously was given to philosophizing—the short, pudgy, oriental woman, pregnant for the twelfth time—they were still in love.

Very much in love.

And Mark Shigata knew by now that in the entire forty-six years of his life he'd never been in love at all. Because he'd looked for all the wrong things. Because there were too many important things his parents, hagridden with a guilt that wasn't theirs at all, had never been able to teach him.

Starting with "Know yourself."

Starting with "Like yourself."

He buried his face in the pillow so he wouldn't disturb Al and Nguyen when he started to cry again.

But he didn't cry.

He slept.

fifteen

SHE'D SEEN HIM AGAIN, ON THE BEACH.

He was hunting her. Just as she'd thought to start with, he was hunting her.

Only it wasn't Dad. It wasn't Dad at all. It was a man who looked a lot like Dad, but it wasn't Dad. She'd gotten close enough to see his eyes, and they were all wrong. They didn't laugh. There weren't any laugh lines running to them. They were like—like black rock, hard and cold.

And they were the wrong shape.

That was who did that in the alley, not Dad. She should have realized that to start with, because Dad left the house that morning wearing a gray suit. He was still wearing a gray suit when he and that other man went in the crummy house. But the man in the alley, the man who'd done that, he was wearing jeans.

She should have known Dad wouldn't do that. She should have told him all about it as soon as he called. Then everything would be all right.

Dad had told her one time how to call home from a coin

phone when she didn't have any money. You dial 0, then the home phone number, then a code. Her code was 4807.

She had been calling off and on all evening. Every time the phone rang and rang and rang, but he never answered. By now it was almost eleven o'clock at night, and he still wasn't there.

He was looking for her, of course. He had to be looking for her. She should have known he'd be looking for her. Looking for her because he cared, not looking for her the way that other man was.

But he couldn't find her and she couldn't find him, and she had to be sure the other man didn't find her.

She had to find a warm place to sleep; it was going to be colder tonight. Even if it hadn't gotten colder she was afraid to go to the beach again. The other man might be there, the one who looked like dad. She had seen him on the beach twice.

And she didn't really even know exactly where she was, much less where she was going to sleep. It's hard to get lost in Galveston, but that was in the daytime. She'd walked all over, tonight.

It had been hours ago that she went trick-or-treating. She had apples, candy, cookies, stuffed in her gym bag, and as she'd hoped, someone had given her hot chocolate. She'd asked for water and they'd given her that too, so she wasn't thirsty. That was good. She'd been thirsty a lot for the last two days.

But she was hungry for *real* food. Something hot. Like a baked potato. Or rice. She liked rice. Dad didn't, so she didn't get it very often.

There had been several kids in the group she'd joined. Then some more kids joined that group, three little kids, she thought they must be Cambodians or Vietnamese or Laotians. There were lots of all of those at school. They seemed like real nice little kids, and one of them had his big brother along to look out for them.

After a while the big brother's cousin came to join them. And then another cousin.

One of the big boys left with the little boys, to take them home he said, but the other two big boys had stayed near her. They hadn't said anything to her, but they hadn't been unfriendly either. They were just there watching. When she came out of the service-station rest room where she'd stopped to wash off her Halloween makeup, both the big boys were helping a little kid air up a bike tire. When she was on the phone at the Seven-Eleven, one of the big boys was playing Donkey Kong on the video machine, and when a drunk man said something to her, some words she didn't understand, the other big boy had walked a little closer to her. He hadn't said anything, but he'd looked at the man and he'd rested his hand on his fish knife.

The man left.

The boy smiled at her and walked a little farther away again.

But he was still there, still near her, like he was protecting her. Like he was her brother. She'd heard the other boys call him Johnnie. Gail wanted to talk to him, but she was scared. It seemed a long time since she'd talked to anybody, except to say trick-or-treat.

She walked along the street, coughing again. She was afraid she was going to start to cry, only she didn't want to because she had used up all her Kleenex. But she was so dirty, and so cold, and so tired, and it seemed like her cold was getting worse, and she kept having this awful feeling that something was bad wrong with her dad.

Johnnie ambled along behind her. The other boy was gone. Now it was just Johnnie. She looked at him.

He smiled at her.

His eyes were like her dad's eyes, only he was a lot younger so there weren't as many smile lines as Dad's eyes had. But he'd made a good start on them.

She smiled at him. A little bit. She didn't mean to, only the smile crawled out.

She was looking at him, and she walked right into a man she didn't even see. She yelped and looked up.

Too far up. He was a very short man.

And his eyes looked exactly like Dad's eyes, all full of smile lines. They were slanted like Dad's eyes, but it was the smile lines she noticed.

"You lost, little lady?" he asked her, and in a funny singing kind of voice. "It mighty late for you to be out."

"Yes," she said in a kind of gasp. "Yes. I—I'm lost. My name is Gail and I tried to call my daddy and he isn't home and I'm scared and—and—"

No doubt about it. She was crying.

"Gail, I am Hoa." He made a funny little bow and gave her a handkerchief, and she giggled through the tears. He smiled. He'd meant her to giggle. "Gail, my little girl is Jacquie. If Jacquie got lost I hope somebody find her and give her supper, yeah? You want to come on my boat all warm and dry, and get some supper?"

Daddy had told her never to go anywhere with a stranger. Never, never, never. But everybody was a stranger and there wasn't anywhere to go—and those eyes—those eyes that smiled—

"Yes," she said, "yes, please—"

It seemed to be a long way to his boat. She went with him and the boy named Johnnie, and there were other boys on the boat. Three of the boys who'd been in the group she went trick-or-treating with. Another boy she'd seen earlier on the beach. They all looked very friendly, and the boat was clean. "These my sons and nephews," Hoa told her. "They all born in United States. Except René, he born in France."

"Why France?" she asked curiously.

Hoa shrugged. "Was where his mama was." All the other boys laughed. René laughed too. Hoa grinned, as if he had made a brand new joke.

"Johnnie, you go call your dad, okay?" Hoa said. "Maybe he can find Gail's daddy, yeah?"

"Maybe he can," Johnnie agreed amiably, and got up from the deck where he had been sitting and walked down that little walkway off the boat.

"Now," Hoa said, "maybe you want a glass of milk, okay? Maybe peanut butter sammich? Maybe rice with fish sauce?"

"Fish sauce?"

"You won't like it," one of the boys told her, in quite unaccented English.

"*You* don't know, I might."

"Get her some, Uncle Hoa," another boy challenged. He rested both elbows on the table and looked at her. "Let's see if she'll eat it. I'll betcha five bucks you won't eat it."

"It's *good*," she said a moment later.

Hoa burst out laughing. "See, Stevie, Gail she know what's good."

"Mr. Hoa—"

"You call me Uncle Hoa, like the boys, okay?"

"Okay. Uncle Hoa, I'll bet my daddy'll get me some fish sauce if I ask. I like fish sauce."

The boy who'd bet she wouldn't like it—Stevie, that was his name—looked astonished, as Uncle Hoa ladled her out another bowlful.

The boy named Johnnie came back on board while she was eating. "Dad's not there," he reported. "Mom said he had to go back out. She said—" He hesitated for a moment and then said something fast in a funny language that sounded like he was singing.

Uncle Hoa looked horrified and answered in the same language, glancing quickly at Gail. The boy named Stevie stood up, eyes blazing and fists clenched at his sides. There was a general stir among the other boys, and one had his hand rested on the hilt of his fish knife just as Johnnie had done earlier.

Uncle Hoa said firmly, "Johnnie's dad will take care of. Gail, she stay here tonight. Tomorrow we find her daddy, okay? Johnnie, you find Gail warm place to sleep. You boys, on deck. Gail will have cabin all to herself."

"But Uncle—" the youngest boy began to protest.

"She girl," Uncle Hoa said severely. "In United States girls more equal than boys, yeah? Johnnie, you get Gail clean clothes. Eddie's jeans, they small enough. Stevie, you get Gail hot water. René, you—"

He stopped.

"Johnnie, you carry Gail to bunk." Gail, curled in a chair, was sound asleep.

* * *

Where do you go when there's nowhere to go?

Sam had promised her if she ever left him he'd kill her. And he would, if he caught her.

But she had to leave him. She had to, because he'd have killed her anyway. He'd have killed her because she wouldn't tell. He'd have killed her just as surely as he killed Wendy, after he followed her to Wendy's house.

Only not as fast as he killed Wendy.

She kept reminding herself that it wasn't her fault. She didn't know he was going to kill Wendy when she went out the back window with Wendy's address book in her purse. And she didn't know he'd follow her to Andrea's house. She didn't know. And she had to run. There wasn't anything else she could possibly do but run.

He'd have killed her. Because he'd finally found out. Found out twelve years late. He'd never noticed before and she didn't know why, unless it was because she was so unimportant to him, so much a part of the background, that he never really looked at her at all. But for some reason he'd suddenly, finally, realized those ripple marks across her abdomen were stretch marks, he'd realized she'd had a baby, and he'd guessed when it happened because that was the only possible time.

If she'd thought fast enough she'd have said the baby was dead. But she didn't think fast enough; she never had thought fast, and she only stared at him, stared stupidly, stared numbly.

She hadn't let him know about the baby when it was born because of Lucie. It was getting hard to remember Lucie now. But she couldn't tell him now, even though the memory of Lucie was fading, because of the boy. The boy.

She started shaking again every time she thought of the boy. Because that was her fault, all her fault.

Lucie wasn't her fault. Sam had said if she ever tried to tell the police about Lucie he'd tell them she'd done it and he'd just helped her cover up. They might believe that. They probably would believe that, because Lucie was Sam's child, not her child. So she never told, even though it wasn't her fault at all.

Lucie. When she remembered Lucie now, what she saw was the picture of Lucie, the picture she kept even though Sam didn't want her to. Lucie laughing, paddling in the wading pool, sunlight in her curly blonde hair forming a nimbus around her face.

Melissa had loved Lucie. Sam couldn't understand that, couldn't understand how she could love another woman's child. But she did.

Sam didn't mean to kill Lucie. She was sure of that. He was hammering a nail and he hit his thumb and he jumped and started cussing. Lucie giggled. She didn't know not to giggle. She was only two years old.

And Sam threw the hammer.

Not at Lucie.

He threw the hammer on the floor and there was a crack in the handle and it split along the crack, and the head of it ricocheted and hit Lucie in the temple.

Sam wouldn't let Melissa take Lucie to the hospital. He said she'd be okay. She'd be okay. She wasn't even crying, she couldn't be hurt bad.

Lucie never cried again.

And two days later Lucie died.

Lucie died and Sam wrapped her in a blanket and buried her in the backyard.

The next one, that wasn't really Sam's fault either. He wasn't drunk. He'd just had a few drinks and he was really tired from working late and honestly he couldn't have stopped, it was a rainy night and the man on the bicycle veered right in front of him and nobody expects to see people on bicycles at two o'clock in the morning.

But Sam did eighteen months in prison for that. They called it driving while intoxicated, and they called it hit and run, and they called it resisting arrest.

It was just after he went into prison that Melissa realized she was pregnant.

Her first thought was utter panic. She wanted the baby, she would love the baby—but—Sam. Sam killed Lucie. And Sam hit Melissa when he was mad at her, or sometimes even when he wasn't mad at her, just for fun. He hit her with that heavy black leather thing he called a sap.

Not the baby. Sam couldn't have Melissa's baby, to hurt it, to kill it.

But she didn't know what to do. Even with Sam in prison she was too afraid to run away from him.

It was Wendy who came up with the idea. She said she was tired of all the pricks. She'd been saying that for months. She said, "Use my name to have the baby. Give me a thousand dollars a month to take care of it. It'll be my baby. You'll be able to see it but Sam won't know."

A thousand dollars was a lot of money, then. The people that worked for Sam didn't make half that. But that was one thing Sam had plenty of, money, and he never asked her how she spent it. He liked to see her dressed up. He'd throw her a handful of bills—big bills—and say, "Don't come back till it's all spent." She never had to keep track of the balance in her checkbook; the bank had orders, if it got low just transfer some more into it.

Things.

She had things.

Wendy had Gail.

But at least Gail was safe from Sam.

Until Melissa decided she wanted a flower bed in the backyard and she didn't think, she'd forgotten where Lucie was buried exactly, she didn't realize the grave was so shallow. She hired that boy who came to the door asking about yard work.

She hired him to dig the flower bed.

And he found the skull. She was standing beside him when he found it; she saw, and knew he saw, how it was crushed, how the hammer had made a hole right through the temple—

He turned to look at her.

She registered appropriate horror. That was easy enough to do. And she said, "It must have been before we bought the house." That was the first thing she thought to say; the boy didn't know Sam had the house built for himself.

"Ma'am, we've got to call the police." The boy was respectful but firm.

If the police were called, they'd know right off who it was. They'd know because Sam had to give some explanation to the neighbors of where the baby went, and so he'd reported Lucie kidnapped. He'd even produced a ransom note.

Enormous relief flooded over her. Maybe she would go to prison, but so would Sam. So would Sam.

"Yes. Yes, you'd better do that. You'd better get the police."

The boy went in the house.

Sam came out. Melissa hadn't known he'd gotten home.

Locked in the bedroom closet, she heard the car started a while later. It was after dark when Sam came back and let her out of the closet and said, "He won't bother us anymore."

Sam finished digging the flower bed. He made Melissa go with him as he took the bones out and dumped them in the bay. Lucie. That was Lucie, all that was left of Lucie, and he dumped it in the bay. Lucie with sunlight in her hair. Dry dusty bones sinking in gray gulf water.

That was the first time he used a whip on Melissa. And he liked it. It made him hot for her.

He said so.

And he did it again, and again.

He quit giving her money, cut off her charge cards. He said she couldn't try on clothes with those marks on her, and obviously she couldn't be trusted with money. She'd proved that when she hired that boy. He'd buy her clothes. She could do her own hair; she didn't need a beauty shop.

She had to call Wendy. She didn't tell Wendy everything, only that she couldn't send any money right now. Wendy said she had to have the money.

Melissa told Wendy to get money from her own husband for a while.

Wendy said she couldn't; her husband didn't *have* that much money. The bills, Wendy screamed, all my clothes—

"Then quit buying clothes for a while," Melissa said.

"I already bought them. The bills—Look, Melissa, I'll

tell you the truth. It's not just that. It's the horses, you know about that, and I owe money to—"

"I'm sorry," Melissa said, "but I haven't got it. I just don't have it. I've given you nearly a hundred and fifty thousand dollars, you can't have spent it all. I'll think of something else soon, I promise."

"You'd better," Wendy said, "because I'm in trouble without it."

You're in trouble, Melissa thought. And she thought, how? How am I going to get a thousand dollars a month now?

It was right after that when Sam started to ignore her, all but one week out of every month. She knew what that meant; it had happened before. It meant he had a girlfriend again.

It wouldn't last. He didn't hit his girlfriends; she knew—she'd been his girlfriend once. So he always came back to her, because he could hit her.

It wouldn't last . . .

Sam liked to play with the whip marks, the one week out of every month he paid attention to her. The old whip marks and the new ones.

It was during one of those weeks that he spotted the stretch marks, almost invisible now, faded to silver, faded so you couldn't see them, but Sam felt them. Sam felt them. And asked. And she didn't answer for just a few seconds too long.

Now there was nowhere to go.

Wendy was dead.

The box, the jewelry box Wendy had given her that she'd hidden all Gail's pictures in, was gone.

Wendy's address book was gone. Or rather, it was at Andrea's house. And Andrea wasn't.

Maybe Andrea wasn't dead. It was still hard to believe what Andrea had told her—that it was Andrea who was Sam's girlfriend this time. Andrea was doing it deliberately, planning some sort of elaborate revenge for all Sam had put Melissa through.

But Andrea didn't know a tenth of what Sam had put Melissa through. Not until that day, when Melissa told her, warned her not to mess around with Sam.

Before that, Andrea had laughed and told Melissa she needed to learn to fight back. After that—after that, Andrea was going to stop him. Somehow. She said so. But now Andrea was gone.

Melissa would have gone to her house anyway, at least long enough to get the address book, but she didn't have a key to the house and she didn't know how to get in without one.

Where do you go when there's nowhere left to go?

It had been a long time since she'd turned a trick. But she guessed she'd healed enough now, it had been a week since last time Sam had hit her, and maybe the johns wouldn't notice. Or care, if they did notice.

She parked her car for a moment on the side of the road, to think about the best place to go.

And suddenly, utterly unexpectedly, she was looking straight at Gail, Gail walking with a man and a teenage boy, Gail looking up eagerly and smiling. She hadn't seen Gail in person since Gail was a year old, since she had given Wendy the extra five thousand dollars and told her to get out of town because Sam was getting out of prison. But she'd had all the pictures Wendy sent her, all those years. All those pictures she'd pored over and cherished and treasured and kept hidden from Sam.

Now she looked fearfully to see who Gail was with, who the man was, who the boy was.

The man was old, Oriental. He looked friendly. He was smiling.

That was no reason to trust him. But instantly, irrationally, she did. Gail was all right. Gail was safe.

She saw them getting on a boat. A shrimp boat, blue, named *Natalie.* It was all right for her to know where Gail was, now, since Sam wasn't around to make her tell.

She picked out a hotel and drove to it, and she walked into the bar standing tall, with a determined smile on her face, and it didn't take her fifteen minutes to find a man willing to pay.

But he wouldn't let her stay in his room all night. Lying relaxed and naked on the bed, he slapped her lightly on the bottom and said, "Sorry, girlie. I been rolled once and that was enough. I paid you. Go find your own place to sleep."

But he hadn't paid her enough. Not enough to get out of town.

Midnight. She had to find another one fast.

Uncomfortable from the sticky wetness in her panties, wishing she had another pair with her, she draped herself on a bar stool and ordered a grasshopper. She looked around hopefully for a man alone. Or a man who could easily be detached from a group of men.

And Sam walked in.

His eyes were glowing, his eyes were the way his eyes looked when he'd been hurting somebody.

He walked straight to her.

Smiling.

sixteen

JIM BARLOW PARKED HIMSELF ON THE ARM
of a chair in Quinn's living room, which was devoid at the
moment of anyone but the three men. "Tell me," he said.
"Everything you can."

"Al, why'd you call in the Bureau?" Shigata picked
crossly at the scrambled eggs Nguyen had brought him
before taking the telephone off the hook and bustling all
the children out into the garden.

Barlow, who had been there drinking coffee in the living room by the time Shigata woke up, leaned forward.
"He was right to call me. This makes it a federal case. You
know that. Assault on a federal officer. I can get in it, now.
And God knows I've wanted in it."

"I guess you want to see." Even he could hear the re-
sentment burning in his voice. Pain, to him, was obscene,
was utterly private; it was disgusting to have to air it in
public as he knew he was going to have to do if the case
ever got into a courtroom. He didn't want to take off the

soft white cotton T-shirt he was wearing and let the special agent in charge see the marks.

"I've got to see. I've got to take photos. Mark, you know that. And from what Quinn tells me, you need to see a doctor."

"If I see a doctor he'll put me in the hospital."

"Probably. It sounds to me as if that's where you need to be."

"I won't go. My daughter—"

Barlow and Quinn exchanged glances. Barlow said, "Your daughter, yes. Well, I'll make a deal with you. You let me take pictures. Tell me what happened. But with you and me and Quinn all able to testify as to your condition, I won't insist you go to a doctor until after Gail turns up, unless you start showing signs of shock or infection. And you've got sense enough to know you've got to have medical help, in that case."

There was a long silence before Shigata said quietly, "Deal."

"Pictures first. Let me get the camera while you get that shirt off . . . holy shit, Mark, he said beating, but I didn't realize—"

"It's not so bad now, except it itches a lot and I know I can't scratch. And muscle soreness of course, I—I was—"

"Yeah. You don't have to tell me that. Just what you saw, what you heard. Anything that will help us identify them. And sometime in the next couple of days you need to get it down on paper for me."

"One name. Sam. Sam looks a lot like me only he's a round-eye. If it wasn't for that he'd practically *be* me from a little distance."

"You didn't tell me that," Quinn said.

"But—" He stopped. "No, I didn't, did I? I just gave you height and weight and coloring."

"Mark," Barlow asked, "could he be Oriental with an eye job?"

A long silence. "He might. Yeah, he might. But—if he is—he—doesn't want to be. He doesn't want anybody to know it. But—maybe—maybe. I'm thinking about the cheekbones, the shape of the mouth, that kind of thing. I don't *know*. I'm inclined to say no because of one thing."

"What's that?" Barlow asked.

"His eyes."

"An eye job—"

"He had *green* eyes," Shigata said. "It wasn't very light there, but I could see that. He had green eyes."

"That sounds pretty conclusive, then," Quinn said. "He's Anglo."

"Maybe not. Because my cousin had green eyes."

"The one you told me about last night?"

"Yeah. That one. I don't remember much about him, but I remember he had green eyes. Just like this guy. But if you did an Identikit we'd come out practically identical except for the eyes."

"You and your cousin?"

Shigata stared at Quinn. "I haven't seen my cousin in thirty years. Me and this guy. This Sam."

Quinn stirred restlessly. "Shigata. Any chance this could *be* your cousin?"

"What?"

"Well, you told me you lost track of—"

"I know I did, but I sure don't see how you could get 'Sam' out of Henry Shigata, do you?"

Quinn shrugged. "It was a thought. But this guy looked a lot like you except for the eyes?"

"That's what I told you. And I got a really good look at him, and I'm not vain enough to spend forty hours a day looking in the mirror but I do shave every morning."

"Mark." Quinn stood up, and Shigata looked at him. He'd figured out last night that when Quinn was calling him by his first name he was getting unusually close to him; the usual last-name address was a form of distancing. Whatever he had to say now was going to be emotionally charged, for one or the other of them. "Mark." Quinn was moving uneasily around the room. "I believe if you think about it, you'll know why Gail ran away."

"Why Gail—"

"Think about it. She looked out the window. She was a ways off from where it happened—that's what, sixty, seventy yards from her bedroom window, a little further from the kitchen window? She looked out whichever window it was and she saw—"

"She saw her daddy killing a woman," Barlow said slowly. "That's what she thinks she saw. That's what—"

"So she didn't call to report it, at first. Then her dad called to say he was going to be late getting home from work, and she didn't understand at all, because he sounded just the same as always, and she didn't dare ask. And she waited, and waited, and waited, and she didn't call the police, because she couldn't call the police and report what she'd seen. But meanwhile there's a body in the backyard, and—"

Shigata sat quite still, as he too realized for the first time what Gail must have seen, what Gail must have thought. But he'd been hit with too much in the last two days;

it seemed this new blow hardly hit him at all. He just sat still in the chair and watched Barlow and Quinn suffer for him.

"There's only one thing to do," Quinn said. "We've got to catch the son of a bitch and print his picture all over the front page. She didn't see his eyes—she couldn't have seen his eyes or she'd know—so she's got to see a paper, she's got to see his face—"

"Suppose we do catch him. What makes you think she'll read the paper?" Shigata asked. "Why do you think that? She's a kid. She doesn't read newspapers. And especially now, hiding, running, running from *me*—"

"She's going to turn up, sooner or later. She's got to turn up, because a twelve-year-old, she can't stay hidden forever. And when she does we've got to make her read the paper, that's all."

"In that case, we'd better have an arrest made so the paper will be ready for her to read," Barlow said. "Keep going, Mark. Everything you can remember."

Shigata shook his head, helplessly, torn now by the shame he hadn't felt while it was happening. "What? I remember hurting. That's all. I remember hurting. I cried, Jim. I cried and I wet my pants and I was so—so—scared I crapped all over myself. I *cried.*"

"So what?" Barlow said. "So you cried. So you lost control of your sphincter muscles. I'd have done the same thing. What else do you *remember,* that's what I need to know."

"Nothing! I remember Sam asking me where Gail was. Over and over. I told you that. And being so angry when I didn't tell him. That's all—Wait a minute. I do remember something else. Just before they left. One of them said something about it being nearly eleven."

"Like he had to be at work, maybe?"

"Yeah. Something like that. And Sam apparently knew about it. He was agreeing. No, that's not right, I take it back. It was the first one said something about he had to leave, and it was Sam interrupted and said something like yeah, he knew, it was nearly eleven."

"You're thinking it was Sam who had to go to work, then?"

"Him or the other guy, the one that was talking. I don't have any idea which. But one or the other."

"Eleven to seven shift? Twelve to eight?"

"I don't know.

"Did they leave early enough to get to work if the shift started at eleven?"

"I don't know. I don't know what time any of it was."

"It was about eleven-fifteen when you called me," Quinn said.

"Okay. If you say so. But I don't know how long I lay on the ground before I called you. I remember—it seems like I kept blacking out. I think I did some moving around when I was semiconscious. I remember the way they had me tied to that bike rack—"

"Tied?" Barlow interrupted. "You sure? Because untying you, that's kinda strange, they don't usually bother. Not if it's rope or something like that. Maybe it was handcuffs and they wanted them back?"

"Yeah. I didn't think about that. You're right." Shigata looked at his wrists. "Handcuffs. I was handcuffed and the chain went through the bicycle rack."

"Have you photographed the rack?" Barlow asked Quinn.

"Uh-uh. Haven't even been to the scene yet. Go on, Shigata."

"Okay, I remember that, and I remember being on the ground, and then I remember hearing Nguyen answer the phone. Nothing at all in between."

"You don't remember going in the house or dialing?"

"Uh-uh. I remember finding my keys and your telephone number. That's all. That was when I was on the ground."

"You may remember later," Barlow said.

"Or he may not," Quinn answered. "Okay, last night you said you recognized some of them as KKK. What about that?"

"Well, the thing is, I don't really think it was a KKK operation."

"No? Sounds like one to me."

"I just don't think it was, and I can't exactly explain why. But for one thing that Sam, whoever he is, definitely is the person who organized the attack on me, and he isn't in our local KKK file at all. I'd have noticed him, or somebody in the office would have, just by the coincidence of him looking so much like me. And if it was a KKK operation the ops officer, so to speak, would have been KKK and he wouldn't have been a new recruit. So I'm thinking it was the same kind of people, some of the same people, but not that organization. And so I don't want anybody to go talk to the ones I recognized. I'll pick them out of the book when I have time, but it's not important because they're underlings. Let them think I didn't recognize them, because if you rock the boat Sam'll bail out. And I don't want him to."

"Well, he hasn't got Gail, anyway," Quinn said.

"He didn't as of last night," Shigata corrected.

"But why in the hell does he want her?" Barlow demanded. "That's what doesn't make sense to me. It didn't when you called me, Quinn, and it still doesn't."

"It would if he was her natural father," Quinn said.

"Twelve years—"

"But if he just now found out," Shigata argued. "He wouldn't even need to want possession of her himself. If you could have heard him last night—gook, slant-eyes, slope-head, Jap bastard—the way he said *'your* daughter'—it would be a matter of—God. Like you found out a cute little puppy had been dragged into a rattlesnake's den. I'm a rattlesnake to him. It was—loathing. Disgust. Me raising a white child. I—am—not—*human* to him, can you understand that?"

"That's sick," Barlow said. "That is so sick. And—it—"

"Okay, it's sick," Quinn shouted. "You think it doesn't exist because it's sick? Live in Shigata's shoes for a while. Hell, live in *my* shoes for a while." He spun around, his back to them, to slam a hard fist into the back of a chair. "The car that hit my boy was eight feet off the road when it hit him, and there weren't any skid marks."

"Al," Shigata said helplessly. "Al."

The ruddy farmer's face turned again to Shigata. "Yeah. I know. I know. Don't hate. But nobody ever said it was easy." He took a deep breath. "For every one like that in the area there's five hundred, more likely five thousand, real people. I know the ones like that are a minority. But they're such a vocal minority. And they do so much damage."

seventeen

"**W**HAT I'M THINKING," BARLOW SAID, "IS that he's some sort of cop. I wish I didn't think that. But I do. It adds up. Handcuffs. Eleven o'clock."

"Cop," Quinn agreed, "or security guard."

"I said some sort of cop. Not necessarily municipal."

"And not necessarily Sam," Shigata said. "Somebody who was there was a cop. I think so too. But I don't think it was Sam. He—I think—I don't know why I think this. But I think Sam has money. And I think he's used to being obeyed. But not as a boss, a supervisor. As somebody who's used to buying people. I don't know why I think that. He was wearing jeans and boots."

"But expensive jeans and boots?"

"Yeah. Something that'd make Tony Lamas look like the nine-ninety-eight special at Kinney's. And a watch. He had—" Memory was coming in dark flashes, bringing with it pain as well as pictures. "It was gold. Heavy. It was—it was—" He shook his head helplessly. "It's gone now. I had it for a minute but it was lost before I could say it."

"Happens," Quinn said, casually dropping a hand on Shigata's forearm for just a second, as Shigata had seen him touch one of his sons earlier in the day.

"Well, let's go have a look at where it happened." Barlow put his cup down and stood up.

"Let me get on a shirt," said Shigata.

"You've got on a shirt."

"A dress shirt. You expect me to work in a T-shirt?"

"I don't expect you to work at all. You're still on suspension."

"Then what am I supposed to be doing?"

"Watching Quinn work, maybe?" Barlow grinned. "Anyhow, I want you to make me one promise. If you start to fall out let somebody know."

"I'll do that."

"Because I've already had to half-carry you twice," Quinn agreed, " and damn it, you're bigger than me."

"Just taller. You're heavier. I'm not going to fall out anyway. Is my tie straight?"

The garage was a dusty useless shell. Not even a whole shell. The roof was almost completely gone, but no sunlight slanted through the holes because the cloud cover was heavy. "November first," Quinn commented. "They call it the day of the dead."

"Who does?" Shigata asked.

"The Mexicans. They have some kind of great big fiesta about it."

"Lots of other people call it that too," Barlow said. "That's what Halloween means, the day before the day of the dead. Not that any of that makes any difference right now. What brought it on anyway?"

"Everything looks so gloomy today. It looks like the day of the dead. I just—this place gives me the creeps. I don't blame you for wanting to tear it down, Shigata."

"It didn't give me the creeps before. It was just in the way. I wanted to put a garden there. Now—" He looked around. "Now I wish we had a hurricane."

Quinn looked at the overhead bicycle rack. "I don't even see how you could reach that."

Shigata didn't answer.

"He didn't have a choice," Barlow said harshly. They could all see where the handcuff chain had scraped a clean rough line across the old metal.

"You had to be on tiptoe," Quinn said. "I can't quite reach it at all."

"I was on tiptoe. I can't reach it either. They looped the chain over. And it was hard to breathe."

"Yeah," Quinn said. "It does something to the position of your lungs, or the muscles that control your lungs, or something like that. Somebody explained it to me but I forgot. You—you didn't tell me they did that to you, Mark." He looked hastily at the ground.

Shigata wondered, briefly, what remembered situation had called up the explanation. He didn't want to know. "Forget it," he said. "We're here to work a crime scene."

Quinn wiped his eyes with his forefinger and thumb. "Yeah," he said. He went on looking at the ground; unwillingly, Shigata's eyes were drawn there too. Barlow was taking pictures of the blood that had dripped down onto the churned sand, along with other biological fluids. "You didn't tell me you puked," Quinn said. He made his tone carefully casual again.

"I didn't remember doing it."

"Somebody puked."

"It was me. I remember now. I just didn't before."

"This must be where you were laying on the ground. If I'd known last night you were bleeding this much I would have called the ambulance whether you wanted me to or not."

"It wasn't much. It just looks like much. Anyway, I eat a lot of liver. Hey, it looks like I dropped—" He knelt. "Those aren't mine."

Barlow, who was still taking pictures, said sharply, "Don't touch it, whatever it is. I'll get there later. Back off, both of you. This is my crime scene. Your garage, but my crime scene."

Quinn and Shigata backed off, Quinn coming when called to hold one end of a ruler, check measurements, initial evidence envelopes. Shigata watched without expression as Barlow collected samples of his blood, his urine, his feces, his vomit. He wondered if the lab would be able to distinguish the tears in the sand.

The gag was a white handkerchief with a blue-and-purple stripe border. He'd vomited on it. They'd jammed it back in his mouth covered with vomit. That thought made him want to vomit again.

But somehow it defused the situation a little, watching Barlow treat it as just another crime scene. Emotionless, calm, methodical. It put a little distance between him and the horror of the night before.

His charcoal gray jacket went into an evidence bag. His starched white shirt. The buttons were ripped off the shirt. That was another thing he didn't remember.

His undershirt was torn. He remembered that. There was a bruise on his neck to remind him.

His tie was in his coat pocket. He'd put it there himself, in Quinn's car, on the way home.

His watch was on the ground. He guessed he'd have to get another one. Evidence can stay impounded a very long time.

Clearly he'd have to get a new one. Someone had stepped on that one.

There were six cartridges spilled on the ground. He checked his gun and found it empty. Returning it to his holster, he felt Quinn's eyes on him. He looked up. "Glad I didn't need it this morning."

"Me, too," Quinn agreed.

At last Barlow had worked his way back to the fallen paper Shigata had spotted. All three men bent over. Photographs, a sheaf of photographs, some marked on the back, all lying face down on the ground. "Don't touch," Barlow repeated. "Good glossy surface like that, there's bound to be prints."

Handling them carefully by the edges, he turned them over one at a time. "Recognize any of them?"

Shigata recognized some of them. They were all of Gail. Mostly of Gail alone. Five of Gail with Wendy. One of Gail with Shigata. And one he'd never seen before of Gail as a tiny baby, held by a woman who fitted the boy's description of Miss Collins's sister.

Shigata could see now what the boy must have meant. Even in this picture, lovingly cuddling the baby, she looked scared.

There were no names on any of the pictures except that

of Gail. But all of them were dated, and on the back of the last one was written, "Gail and me."

They had known fingerprints of Gail's mother, the woman they were calling Wendy-two. And from the hospital they had been able to obtain some old samples of her handwriting. Shigata by now was suspecting she might be the Melissa they were hunting.

The lab would be able to determine whether the woman who had written "Gail and me" on the back of that picture was the woman who had filled out those forms at the hospital. And, possibly, whether those were her fingerprints on the picture. Andrea Collins's neighbor could tell whether that was the woman they'd been told was Andrea's sister.

They might now be well on their way to finding Melissa, Melissa who—maybe—could break the whole thing open. Melissa who—maybe—could help them find Gail.

Barlow collected the photos delicately with tweezers, putting each one into separate evidence bags.

Shigata looked longest at the picture of the unknown woman. But Barlow looked longest at the picture of Shigata, before sliding it too into an evidence bag, stapling the bag shut, and writing his initials on it.

"I want Mrs. Watson to look at this one picture," Quinn said suddenly. Evidently his thoughts were running parallel to Shigata's.

"Later." Barlow stood up. "Mark, I'll need the clothes you were wearing last night, whatever you still had on when you got inside."

"I spread them in the bathroom to dry some," Quinn told him. "Figured you'd want them."

Shigata didn't say anything. He knew it was necessary.

That didn't help his emotional state any. Impotent rage, helpless fury, were eating a hole in his stomach.

He followed them into the house, wondering when Quinn had taken possession of his keys. He took cartridges out of a box in the desk and slammed them into the cylinder of his revolver.

He watched passively as Barlow folded his trousers and undershorts, put them into paper bags, and labeled the bags "clothing of victim," marking them also with the date, time, and a case number. Barlow proceeded then to take possession of even the socks and shoes he'd been wearing the day before.

He wondered when a case number had been assigned.

He wasn't used to being "victim." He wasn't used to being a case number.

It was a depersonalizing experience. And he shied like a spooked horse when Quinn casually rested a calloused hand high on his shoulder.

"You okay?" Quinn asked him.

"No. But I'll make it."

Quinn nodded and turned away.

Shigata hoped he'd make it. There were intense recurring muscle spasms over his whole body, especially his arms and the sides of his chest and abdomen where he had been stretched up to reach the handcuffs. His back was hot and throbbing, and secretly he was beginning to fear the onset of infection. At least his tetanus shots were current, he assured himself. But he was thirsty and he was hurting, and he was so tired it felt almost like physical impossibility to keep going. He knew what he needed. He needed a massive dose of penicillin, and he needed a good strong painkiller and a good strong muscle relaxer, and he needed rest.

A lot of rest.

Barlow found a thermometer in the medicine chest and turned around and handed it to him. "If it's over a hundred and one I call an ambulance," he said conversationally. "And you keep it in your mouth the full three minutes. I'm timing it."

It was a hundred and eight-tenths. He'd have gone to a doctor to get penicillin, only he was afraid the doctor would promptly load him up with some kind of dope and put him in a hospital whether he wanted to go there or not.

He was hoping things would progress fast, before he had time to get really sick.

"Check it again in a couple of hours," Barlow said. "Pain is one thing. It's your problem. If you want to try to ignore it, go right ahead, and more power to you. But that's a massive open wound and you haven't had a thing on it but peroxide. And you can't afford infection."

He wondered how Barlow knew about the peroxide. But Quinn was looking guilty; Quinn must have told him. "I'll watch the temperature," he said. "Don't worry. I'm not planning on dying." Barlow was right. He couldn't afford to ignore infection.

"Don't let him forget," Barlow told Quinn.

"He told you he'll check it," Quinn said.

"Okay. Well, I'm going into Galveston and see what they can do about latents on these photos. As soon as they've checked that one of the woman I'll get them to make some prints of it for you. But I think the latents are what we need. If this Sam, whoever he is, has any kind of a record, the latents *will* be all we need. Where will you two be?''

Quinn had his mouth open to answer. Shigata forestalled it. ''Quinn's office, for a while. We need to figure out exactly what we can do about finding Melissa. I've got a hunch Melissa, when she's turned up, can tell us exactly who—and where—Sam is. After that, I don't know.''

''We can take a walkie-talkie with us,'' Quinn offered. ''That way my office will be able to find us.''

It was the second time Shigata had been in the Bayport Police Station.

This time, trying not to let himself worry about Gail— because they were doing everything they could to find Gail, and his head knew it even if his stomach didn't—he made a conscious effort to imagine himself running this police department. It gave him a surprisingly good feeling, and without thinking what he was doing, he began to ask Quinn questions.

Dispatch, four civilians, three shifts and one relief. Really need one more, he thought. The dispatchers were also doing the night typing and filing, although there was a clerk in the daytime on weekdays. Tape machines with automatic timers; all incoming calls and all radio messages were taped. Good. This size department, that had to be a federal grant. Small muster room, small locker rooms. Holding cells, only two of them; prisoners would be moved quickly to the Galveston County Jail.

File drawers for reports, centralized: investigative, traffic, and miscellaneous all went in together. Not exactly ideal, but okay, considering the size of the department. A very small fingerprint file. Minimal evidence-collection facilities, but for anything big they'd ask for help from Galveston anyway.

Room for two investigators, although Quinn was the only one right now, and normally the chief also served as investigator. But the acting chief they had right now was working with uniform division.

Such as it was right now. Shigata's mind balked at the idea of the chief of police writing traffic tickets.

If Quinn guessed why Shigata was asking so many questions he didn't comment. He was digging through some old city directories, and he glanced up when Sergeant— now acting chief—Dan Buchanan came in.

Glanced up and froze, because Shigata stood up fast with his hand on his gunbutt, and when Buchanan's hand started toward his own pistol Shigata, without drawing, said, "I wouldn't try, bastard." And Buchanan stood very still and very slowly raised his hands.

"Quinn, disarm him," Shigata said, a deadly stillness in his voice.

Quinn walked carefully around the side of the room, not getting between the two men, and took Buchanan's service revolver out of its holster.

eighteen

"I'M NOT GOING TO TELL YOU WHO SAM IS. I'll tell you whatever else you want to know, but I won't tell you who Sam is." He was sitting back comfortably, the self-satisfied smirk on his face belying his empty holster.

"If you'll tell us everything else, why won't you tell us who Sam is?"

"You're standing there feeling like you've got to be feeling and asking me why I won't cross Sam?"

"We're going to get him, one way or another."

"You do that. You get him, if you can. But not with my help. I say you can't anyway. And I say you can't do anything to me. I'll be sitting back there in my own office when you're pushing up daisies."

Shigata took a deep breath. "Did Sam kill Andrea Collins?"

"I ain't gonna tell you what Sam did. Anyway I don't know if Sam killed Andrea Collins. I wasn't there."

"Do you know who Andrea Collins was?"

"Yeah, I know who Andrea Collins was. She's the bitch that—" He stopped abruptly.

"She's the bitch that what? What were you going to say, Buchanan?"

"Nothing, Shigata. I wasn't going to say."

"I notice you didn't need anybody to tell you who I am."

"I know who you are. You're that goddamn dink fed, that's who you are. Your name's Shigata. You was hassling Short and Monahan."

"Hassling Short and Monahan?" Quinn repeated.

"Yeah, Al, I was hassling Short and Monahan," Shigata agreed wearily. "I was interfering with their Godgiven right to burn shrimp boats they didn't like the owners of."

"Look, they come over here and take our jobs! We gotta defend ourselves!"

Shigata put his hands in his pockets and turned away. "You a shrimp fisherman, Buchanan?"

"No, I'm not a damn shrimp fisherman."

"Then I don't guess anybody's taken your job. At least not yet." He pulled a chair out and rested one foot on it. "But one sure thing, somebody's going to, because you're going to federal prison."

"Only if you live to testify, crybaby."

Shigata caught Quinn's fist just in time. *"No,"* he said forcefully. "We handle it legally. Otherwise we're as bad as he is."

Buchanan leaned back in the chair, long legs sprawled under the table. "The reason I don't care what I tell you," he stated, "is because you'll never live to tell about it." He glanced between Quinn and Shigata; then his gaze shifted to Quinn. "You neither, gook lover. Why the mayor let you get hired onto this department I'll never know.''

"How'd Wendy's jewelry box get in my backyard with Andrea's body?''

"I don't know nothing about Wendy's jewelry box. There was Melissa's—'' He stopped again.

"Melissa's what? Melissa's jewelry box? Maybe a box with a butterfly on the lid?''

"Yeah, that was Melissa's.'' Clearly he hadn't meant to say Melissa's name. But he'd already said it, and he couldn't take it back.

"So that was Melissa's. How'd it get in my backyard?''

"I don't know.''

"Then you don't know much, do you, asshole?'' Quinn asked.

"I know more than you do, motherfucker.'' Buchanan had hardly moved a muscle. Now he looked up, grinning, and began to light a cigarette.

Quinn took the cigarette out of his hand.

Shigata moved the package out of his reach.

Somewhere in the building a door closed. The clock ticked off twelve seconds.

Buchanan shrugged. "So I don't smoke. I still know more than you do.''

"Prove it. You said you'd tell about everything but Sam. How'd the jewelry box get in my yard?''

"I told you I don't know. It was Melissa's. Sam told me to get it. And get Melissa too, if I could. I couldn't find Melissa. I got the box but Melissa got away. She had to be there—her suitcases were there and her car was out in front, but she got away. I couldn't find her. Sam was plenty mad. Give me a cigarette.''

Shigata put the cigarettes in his pocket.

"Please. Hear me? I said please, real pretty."

"So did I. Last night."

"Look, I didn't do that! That wasn't me! That was Sam. You just don't dare cross Sam. Man, I'm telling you—"

"I hear you. You gave the jewelry box to Sam. Did he open it then?"

"Yeah, he opened it then. He put the pictures in his pocket and he threw the box in his car seat."

"Where did all this happen? And when?" Shigata took the cigarettes out of his pocket.

Buchanan's gaze shifted. "I can't tell you that."

Shigata put the cigarettes back in his pocket. "Then let's talk about the address book. Know anything about it?"

"Not much. Sam thought maybe Melissa might have took it to Andrea's house, after he figured out Wendy didn't have it. So he told me to go ask Andrea for it real nice. He was—he couldn't go see her himself right then."

"Saving her for later?" drawled Quinn.

"You could say that," Buchanan said. "But anyhow, I went and asked for it. So Andrea said she wasn't going to let Sam have it. She said she was tired of Sam."

Quinn and Shigata exchanged glances. *Tired* of Sam? That seemed to suggest a relationship between Andrea and Sam. And Shigata's mind made the leap. Andrea had a new boyfriend. She wanted to get even.

For what?

"Andrea told me she was going after school to return it to Wendy. So I knew right off Melissa couldn't have told her Wendy was dead. So I said she didn't know where Wendy lived and I could take it. She said she did know. She said Wendy had told her a year ago. So I knew from that she meant Wendy's old address. So when Sam got—when I saw Sam I told him."

"And Sam met her there and killed her."

"I guess. I wasn't there."

"What about Andrea's car?"

"Well, Sam told me to get it." He seemed very disinclined to explain where he had put it.

Shigata decided not to press the matter at the moment. He put the cigarettes back on the table. "Why the attack on me?"

Eyeing the cigarettes, Buchanan said, "Well, it wasn't until Saturday when he had time to really study the pictures that he realized it was you who had his kid. Thing is, he hadn't seen Wendy in about fourteen years. He didn't know—Well—"

"Well, what? He didn't know what?"

"Well, see, he knew Wendy had got married. But he didn't know who to. I guess Melissa had tried pretty hard to keep him away from Wendy. So he didn't know it was Wendy had his kid. I mean, he did know Wendy had married a gook—man, that really made him sick, you know it, I think he kinda had the hots for Wendy some himself—and he knew there was a kid, because sometimes Melissa would send stuff to the kid, casual-like. But I guess he thought it was the gook's kid. He didn't know till he looked at the picture it was a white kid. And that was when he knew it had to be his."

"How'd he know that?" Quinn asked. "Why couldn't it just have been Wendy's kid?"

"Oh, Wendy couldn't have any kids," Buchanan said casually. "She had an abortion when she was sixteen and got real sick and almost died and they had to do some kind of operation to keep her from dying. So it couldn't be Wendy's kid. And see, he knew Melissa had a kid—he'd just found that out, and that was what all the fighting and stuff was about, because Melissa wouldn't tell him where the kid was, and then he saw that picture of Melissa with the kid, and Wendy with the kid, and then the gook with the kid.'' He stared at Shigata, disgust in his eyes. ''Sam tells me everything. You got no business raising Sam's kid. You got no business with any white kid. But especially not Sam's kid. Sam wants her back.''

''Sam never had her to start with.''

''Tell that to Sam.'' Buchanan casually picked up the cigarettes. Quinn and Shigata didn't stop him.

He was looking straight between Shigata and Quinn, smiling. He lit a cigarette, took a deep breath, looked startled, and started to rise. There was a harsh cough. Almost simultaneously he released his breath in a curious sigh and flopped backward in the chair, his head slinging back and then falling forward. Blood and something else sprayed on the table.

Shigata ran for the front hall. There was nobody in sight. He flung open the front door. The street was empty. Back inside the building. The men's room. The women's room. Empty. He grabbed at the door to the municipal court room. Locked. The door to the supply room. Locked. The evidence room. Locked.

Of course all the doors were locked; it was Sunday. Of course all the doors in a small-town city hall were locked. What else could he expect?

He burst back into the office complex, shouting, ''Have you got a key to any of those doors?''

''Uh-huh.'' Quinn was still bending over Buchanan's

body. "He does, though." He began to rifle through pockets. "What the hell? All I heard was a cough."

"That was no cough, that was a silencer. Turn him, check that other pocket, they've got to be somewhere."

Quinn found the keys and let the body flop to the floor. "Why him and not us?"

"Because Sam's still hoping one of us'll lead him to Gail. Which key goes to what?"

"Danged if I know. Shigata—"

"Just stay there. Call the ME if you haven't already." Sixteen keys. With a little struggling and swearing he got all the locked doors open. And the rooms checked, and the doors relocked.

But he'd lost three minutes hunting keys. Plenty of time for someone who knew the building to get away.

"Who's your ranking officer now?" he asked Quinn.

"Me. Everybody else is junior to me." Quinn was still photographing the corpse. "Shigata, I'm telling you, there is nobody who has keys to this building named Sam, and there's nobody who looks like you. I'd know."

"Well, he sure as hell didn't shoot himself." Shigata looked with extreme displeasure at the body. "You got the medical examiner coming?"

"I got the ME coming."

"He wasn't going to tell us."

"Apparently Sam didn't know that. Whoever in the hell Sam is. Your back's bleeding again."

"The hell with my back. I've got other things on my mind."

"Shigata. What are we going to do now? What in the goddamn bloody hell do we do now?"

"Exactly what we were going to do. Find Melissa."

nineteen

I T WASN'T UNTIL MEDICAL EXAMINER'S INVES-
tigator Bob Mann arrived to pronounce Buchanan dead—
a rather foregone conclusion, with the back blown out of
his head by the bullet now lodged in the detective bureau
wall—that Quinn and Shigata realized Dan Buchanan had
set up his own murder.

Not that he'd meant to, of course. Not that he'd thought
that was what he was doing. He'd thought he was setting
up Quinn and Shigata.

"He picked the chair himself," Quinn remembered.
"Neither of us told him where to sit. He just—sat down,
and we were both standing, facing him. He was facing the
outside door, and we had our backs to it."

"I wonder—" Shigata strode into the chief's office, a
glass-fronted room opening onto the tiny detective bureau, and walked behind the desk, examining its surface.
"Al," he said. "Mann. Come here."

The desk calendar was open to the double page marking

Saturday October 31/Sunday November 1; written on Sunday's page, in pencil, was "Sam 9:15."

"He knew Sam was coming," Shigata said. "So when I spotted him all he had to do—he thought—was turn us with our backs to the door and then run out the clock. Sam would take care of the rest. He thought. Wonder why Sam didn't kill us?"

"He wants us—you, at least—alive," Quinn reminded him. "So you can lead him to Gail. But damn it, killing Buchanan like that—"

"He was through with Buchanan, I guess," Shigata said.

"Anyhow, he must've known Sam was coming armed," Quinn said thoughtfully. "Buchanan, I mean. Buchanan must've known—"

"I'd agree, if it wasn't for the silencer," Shigata said. "Think about it. You and I walk around armed, but nobody carries a silencer around with him. Damn things are bulky. Besides, it was closer to nine-thirty that Buchanan was shot. No, I think Sam came in, saw what was happening, and went back to get his pistol. And Buchanan must have known he would. What I can't figure out is how he got away so fast. Al, who would have keys to this building, to those locked rooms? I mean, not every patrolman in this department has them, right? You didn't."

"I have keys to where I'm authorized to go alone. I don't need to be able to get a machine gun out of the supply closet. I do have keys to the evidence locker, but not to the municipal courtroom. Anyhow, think it through. It's just about as likely somebody would have a pistol with a silencer so close he could go and get it and be back in fifteen minutes as it is that he's still walking around the streets carrying it. Shigata, it just doesn't make sense. Any of it."

"Damn it, Quinn, it happened," Shigata said. "So somebody's bound to—"

"All right. Keys. The acting chief. He's sitting over there dead. The mayor. Jolene Robinson. She's five-feet-six and redheaded and I don't think anybody could mistake her for you, and furthermore, despite Buchanan's yap about her letting me in the department, she's a straight-shooter. I mean—"

"I hear you. You're not talking guns. Go on."

"The city manager. Bob Crowley. He's six-four, two hundred eighty pounds, and a Jolene Robinson hire. That's what precipitated that last round of firings and resignations, by the way. The city manager before Crowley hassled Cal Woodall—Chief Woodall—into quitting. Woodall was one straight arrow. Dale Shipp replaced him, and I kid you not, when Shipp dies they're gonna have to screw him into the ground. Then the last city election, they got a whole new city council and mayor—that's when Jolene got elected—and they fired the old city manager and had a good search for a new one. When they finally hired Crowley he sat and watched for a while and then fired Shipp. If my candidate don't run I'll cast my vote for Woodall coming back. Look, what the hell difference does it make about the keys? I mean, if Buchanan knew he was coming then Buchanan had to know he could get in, right? For all I know, Buchanan might have give him the keys."

"You're probably right," Shigata muttered.

"What's all the discussion about keys?" Mann asked. Without waiting for an answer, he went on, "Hey, Quinn, just when did you get to vote for chief of police anyway?"

Quinn shrugged. "I don't. But if I could I would. Except I don't think Woodall wants to come back. Mann, you got everything you need?"

"Yeah, unless you want to tell me who shot him."

"Somebody named Sam. Caucasian. About five-ten, a hundred and sixty pounds, black hair, brown eyes, dark complexion."

"Gospel or guess?"

"Educated guess."

"That don't cut no onions with the DA's office when it comes to taking warrants," Mann told him.

Quinn shrugged. "We don't know who the hell Sam is anyway."

"Terrific." Mann got on his walkie-talkie and told his office to send somebody to transport the body. Then he turned to Quinn and Shigata. "You got the bullet out of the wall yet?"

"Uh-huh," Quinn said. "You want to do the honors?"

"Not particularly."

"Look, we might better get Galveston to do it," Quinn said nervously. "I mean, I never tried to get a bullet out of a wall before and I sure don't want to mess up the fire-arms evidence."

Shigata unfolded his pocketknife. "It's real simple," he said. "You just don't scratch the slug, that's all."

Mann, behind him, said, "Hey, mister, how'd that blood get on the back of your shirt?"

"I guess it grew there."

"Al, your brother-in-law's on the phone." The dispatcher looked about sixteen. She also looked extremely frightened. "At least I guess it's your brother-in-law. I can't understand him."

"I'll call him later."

"But—"

"Do I look like having time to talk to my brother-in-law? Tell him I'll call back later."

"We could check county records and find out who Melissa Blair married," Quinn suggested.

"We could if it wasn't Sunday and if we knew for sure whether she was married in Galveston County or Harris County or Hong Kong or Zanzibar."

"Oh. Yeah. Well, we could—"

"Quinn."

"Yeah?"

"Where do you keep your search warrant forms?"

Shigata had stopped to get his jacket; he was tired of being told about the blood on his shirt, and besides that, the gray day had begun to spit occasional halfhearted drizzles of rain.

It had taken a little while to track down a judge to sign the search warrant, but there had been no problem with getting it issued. A dead woman, found away from her house, not identified until over twenty-four hours later. Middle of three (sort of) sisters. Older sister dead in her own apartment. Younger sister likely threatened, possibly dead too.

Younger sister could be located only by finding middle sister's address book, as her address was not in older sister's book.

Which probably said something, Shigata mused as Quinn drove back toward Prune Street. But he wasn't sure what it said. All he was sure of was that no Melissa, no Sam, and no one named Blair showed up in Wendy's address book or in Shigata's address book that Wendy in the past had sometimes used.

The warrant specified address books, diaries, other papers that might show next of kin, relationship to the other victim, and knowledge of a suspect believed to have the first name of Sam.

It was a small house, from the outside. But there was a surprisingly large area where papers might be. "We want to make damn sure we're absolutely covered," Shigata said. "Witness to everything."

"Can't we not do it and say we did?"

"No, we can't not do it and say we did," Shigata answered. "I don't know about you, but I don't lie on the witness stand."

There was a long silence before Quinn said, "Well, come to think of it, I don't either."

"Good. Because I guarantee you, if your horse does decide to run, you won't."

"Okay."

"Al, you've got to understand this. If I do decide to apply for that job—and if I should happen to get it—I'll *be* chief of police."

The door popped open, under the pressure of Quinn's foot at the lock plate. After regaining his balance, Quinn answered, "That's the general idea." His gaze met Shigata's. "I know I fuck up sometimes. But I have to respect a man before I can take having him tell me I fucked up. I'd have taken it from Woodall. I'd take it from you—hell, I *do* take it from you. You know I do. But if Shipp hadn't got fired when he did I'd have quit. Or killed him, one or the other. Because I wouldn't take it from him.''

"If you think I'm fucking up, you tell me.''

"I will. Come to think of it, I do.''

Shigata chuckled. "You do, don't you? Okay. Witness to everything.''

That meant they couldn't separate to search, and it meant the job was going to take twice as long as it otherwise would. Shigata would search while Quinn watched, and Quinn would search while Shigata watched.

The house was small. Andrea's kitchen and living room belonged to the mathematics teacher. The kitchen was all geometric shapes; it could have come from a glossy women's magazine or from a chemistry laboratory. She apparently delighted in the interplay of shapes, textures, and colors: different shapes of pasta were lovingly arranged in closed apothecary jars and chemical beakers, and hanging wire baskets held red onions, scarlet chili peppers, limes, lemons.

But at closer glance the pasta was old and darkened; the onions, peppers, and limes were plastic. Only the lemons were real and they were beginning to mold.

There were no papers in the kitchen at all, except for two cookbooks.

Two small cookbooks.

Food, apparently, was not the area of Andrea's greatest interest.

The living room was as clean as the kitchen. It had a waxed wood floor with no scatter rugs, a love seat rather than a couch, one wall-hugging recliner chair upholstered to match the love seat. There was a small television set sitting on an end table. Another end table was set up as a bar; partial bottles of vodka, bourbon, and Scotch; glasses; assorted bar tools.

A thin film of dust overlay it all, but it wasn't old dust; probably it had gathered since Thursday night, presumably the last time anyone had used this room.

The small desk had a fluorescent lamp on it, and a pair of book ends supported four mathematics books, a dictionary, a zip-code book, and a college catalog. Lap drawer. Pens, pencils, scissors, envelopes, stamps, paper clips, staples and stapler. Top left drawer, three years' worth of bank statements. Shigata's hand hovered over them; his gaze shifted back to the search warrant and, reluctantly, he withdrew his hand and closed the drawer.

He looked at Quinn and shrugged. "There's not going to be any names there. If she got any checks from Sam, we can't tell it by her bank statement. And there won't be any checks to Sam. It's not covered by our warrant." He glanced again at the closed drawer. "But if I can think of any probable cause, I might go back and get another warrant."

"You went into Wendy's house without any warrant at all. Why so finicky now?"

"Al, I was still legally *married* to Wendy. I'll admit I didn't go to law school in Texas, but I'll bet there's no law says I couldn't go into her place with or without her permission."

"Well."

"Yeah. I know. It was only technically legal. Because I was entering as law enforcement officer, not as husband. But all the same I'm pretty sure it *was* technically legal." He turned again to his task.

Middle left drawer. Unexpectedly, an assortment of

hardware. A hammer. Not a very good one. Several screw-drivers, both slot and Phillips head. Picture hanging wire, plant hooks, molly-bolts. Apparently she'd been planning to put up some hanging plants. But that was none of their business.

Bottom left drawer. Address book. Shigata collected it, wrote it down on the search warrant, but resisted the temptation to open it immediately. Under it, a Christmas card list. He hesitated and then collected it also.

Top right drawer. A box of Kleenex. A bottle of Tylenol. Vitamin C, vitamin B. Not completely out of character, a bottle of Valium. "Wonder why she kept that stuff there?" Quinn mused.

"No telling," Shigata said.

What looked like two lower drawers on the right turned out to be a single file drawer. File jackets on, apparently, every student she had that year. Very methodical, was Andrea.

A file jacket labeled "Bills." Shigata hesitated, then picked it up and looked through it. He put it back in the drawer and closed the drawer.

The bedroom was not the mathematics teacher's room. A quilted wall hanging of a unicorn prancing out of a rain-bowed forest hung shining on one wall; it appeared to be of pure silk, and neither Quinn nor Shigata was prepared to guess at the cost of it. The satin-covered king-size bed, piled high with satin cushions in jewel colors, sat in a little alcove, and both walls and ceiling of the alcove were mir-rored. The drawer of a bedside table held a collection of adult toys that made even Shigata, who for one memorable year had taught the FBI sex-crime school to area police departments, blink; Quinn was frankly agape.

But he closed the drawer and turned to Shigata with a grin. "Anybody who needs those has got problems."

"Some people have problems," Shigata returned.

The dresser held lingerie. Andrea's lingerie was more appropriate to the rich man's mistress she was at night than to the math teacher she was in the daytime, and some of it, to both men, looked frankly miserable to think of wearing. Quinn picked one garment up. "What the hell do you suppose it is?"

"I don't know what you call it," Shigata said doubtfully. "I think it's to make her waist look smaller and her bosom look bigger. Like a Playboy bunny wears."

"And I don't see how they walk in those things."

"I asked one once, though, and she said actually they're fairly comfortable until they've been on too long. Well. This is getting nowhere." He closed that drawer.

There were no papers of any kind in the dresser, but in one drawer they did find some more practical underwear. "I didn't think she'd want to waste that twenty-dollar lace on a classroom desk," Shigata said.

The dressing table held cosmetics. Not, oddly enough, a lot of cosmetics. Quinn didn't recognize the brand; Shigata did. "Neiman-Marcus is the only local distributor I know of. I don't know how much all of it costs. The makeup base is about thirty-six dollars and the lipstick is twelve-fifty. I forgot the rest. Wendy used the same brand. I was with her one time when she bought it; that's how I know."

"That's a sin," Quinn said firmly, and Shigata laughed.

There were two closets in the room. One was the math teacher clothing; the other belonged to the high-class whore.

Still no more papers.

There was a big storage closet off the kitchen. And it was piled high with papers. Very neatly boxed papers.

Both men jumped violently as the radio on Quinn's belt came alive. "Your brother-in-law wants you to call him," said the dispatcher's rather nervous voice.

"Tell my brother-in-law I'm busy," Quinn said. "I'll call him at lunchtime."

Shigata had been opening one of the boxes. Now he whistled softly, and Quinn turned. Shigata handed him one of the papers. He looked at it. "All the same?" he asked.

"I haven't checked all the boxes. But yes, I think they're going to be all the same. I think she was storing them for Sam."

There was nothing to show where, or by whom, the papers had been printed. Volume 4, number 11, it said at the top. November. The papers were waiting to be shipped, but no address labels had been affixed. The name of the paper was *Sons of Liberty*. Shigata considered that tantamount to blasphemy.

Because the paper was a blatant appeal to race hatred. Whatever organization had printed it—presumably, something that had decided to call itself by a noble two-hundred-year-old name—hated Blacks. Hated Latin-Americans. Hated Orientals. Hated Indians. Hated Jews. Hated Catholics. Was obsessed with fear of any kind of sexual union that might produce such a mongrel race. Was quite sure such a union was the deliberate attempt of some vast unnamed conspiracy apparently jointly run by the Pope, the president of the Mormon church, and the Zionists.

The typesetting was neat and professional. To Shigata, the illustrations were almost—but unfortunately not quite—obscene.

He took the paper out of Quinn's hand and laid it neatly back in the box he'd taken it out of.

"What are you going to do about it?" Quinn asked, resisting the impulse to scrub his hands against his pants legs.

"Nothing," Shigata said. "It's not illegal. Let's get the hell out of here."

twenty

"**W**ELL, THERE'S NO SAM IN THIS ONE, EI-ther," Quinn said.

The detective bureau—such as it was—had been cleaned up by persons unknown, but Quinn and Shigata by unspoken agreement were not using it. They were both in the chief's office, where Shigata, without saying a word, had slung the dead man's personal property into a cardboard box before sitting down behind the desk to begin to go through Wendy's address book again. Quinn, his chair drawn up to the front of the desk, had been going through Andrea's.

"Okay," Shigata said, "next step. Let's compare both books, page by page. We've fairly well established a minimum of contact between the two for a long time, so anybody who shows up in both books will at least go back a long way."

That took over an hour. Wendy and Andrea were in each other's address books. But there was nobody at all who appeared in both books. Apparently both women either knew Melissa's address too well to have to write it down, or had broken off contact with Melissa entirely.

"What now?" Quinn asked. "Do we start calling everybody in both books?"

"Only if we have to." Shigata stood up. Every time he sat still for very long his back began to stiffen. He hoped Quinn couldn't read his face as well as he was afraid Quinn could read his face, because the pain was rising toward a peak again and he didn't know how far up that peak was going to be. Every beat of his pulse was a fresh wave of heat; he knew he was sweating and hoped there wasn't a thermometer in the building, so Quinn couldn't decide to check his temperature.

He looked around. Quinn was watching him with quiet sympathy. "I'm not hiding a thing from you, am I?" he asked wryly.

"Uh-huh. I told you, I've been there. I've got some aspirin if you think that'll help any."

"Does it?"

"Don't know. I didn't have any then. But on the other hand I wasn't trying to work, either."

"Yeah, I'll try it." Aspirin. A water fountain. Awkward. Another cup of coffee. Too hot. A Coke out of the machine in the hall.

"We could go back through the address books and see if we can find anything that looks—say—incongruous," Shigata suggested.

"Incongruous how?"

"Just—unlikely. Like a stockbroker in Wendy's. That sort of thing."

"Oh, Wendy didn't screw stockbrokers?"

"You know what I mean."

"Yeah. Okay, let's give it a shot." Ten minutes later he said, "Shigata."

"Yeah?"

"I've got a gun shop. No name for it, it just says 'gun shop.' But it's under *S.* What would Andrea want with a gun shop?"

Shigata laid down Wendy's book. "I don't know. Give it to me. I didn't see any guns at her house, did you?"

"Uh-uh. And I was looking. I don't care what the search warrant says, I *always* look for guns. I want to know what's likely to be turned against me. What are you doing?"

"Dialing. What does it look like I'm doing?"

"You expect to find a gun shop open on Sunday morning?"

"Uh-uh. But I just want to be able to say I tried . . . Yes, operator, I'm Mark Shigata with the Federal Bureau of Investigation. I have a telephone number here and I urgently need to know who it belongs to. Can you—All right, then, may I speak to your supervisor? Then when will she be off break? Is there any other supervisor I can—Oh, I see. No, I—Yes, I know what the Federal Communications Act of nineteen thirty-four says, and I think you'll find that refers to secrecy of *communications,* not—Miss, this is an extremely urgent investigation—*Bitch!*" He had hung the phone up before he said that.

"They don't like to give 'em out," Quinn agreed. "And it's the wrong time of day. The supervisors like to go on break in the middle of the morning. Why don't you try back about eleven?"

"Yeah, I guess," Shigata said. "Okay, then, while we're waiting, let's try and see if we can figure out where he went after killing Buchanan." He headed for the front door, Quinn following him, and went and stood on the front steps and looked out at the street. "What's here?" he asked.

Quinn, beside him, gestured to the left. "Fire station. To the right, water department. This whole block is city offices. And I know—not necessarily by name, but at least by sight—every person who works in them. I'm telling you, Shigata, it was not a city employee."

"I'll take your word for it. All right, across the street."

"I need to tell you?"

"Uh-uh." Rains and Slappey Funeral Home took up more than half the block, from the corner to past the center. Beside that, a small storefront building that featured K&S Sporting Goods, and an office supply store with a small sign saying *Bayport Sentinel*.

"What's the *Bayport Sentinel*?" Shigata asked.

"A small-town weekly newspaper that wants to grow up and be the *National Enquirer,* only it'll never make it. I don't read it. I did once and that was enough. It was founded as a hobby by some guy I've never met. They tell me he got rich off oil money and then lost his business."

"Lost his business how?"

"It got expropriated by some Arab state that decided to nationalize everything. Didn't hurt him much personally, he's still got plenty of money, but he's no JR anymore, and they tell me he sure did love to play JR."

"Tough shit. What about K&S Sporting Goods?"

"It's mainly—" Quinn stopped and then repeated, slowly, "It's mainly a gun shop. But Shigata, it's run by a guy named Bob Kerns who's as nice a fellow as you'd ever hope to meet. I've known him about ten years."

"Let's check the phone numbers, anyway."

Shigata wasn't even surprised when the telephone book matched Andrea's scrawled telephone number. "Call Kerns," he told Quinn.

"He'll be at church."

"Not necessarily. We're not. Call Kerns."

Quinn picked up the phone. "Hello, Bob? Al Quinn. I'm on a pretty urgent investigation, you mind if I—yeah, I do need your help. You mind if I come out and talk with you for a few minutes—Well, I'll tell you when I get there. I'll have another man with me; he's an FBI agent. Yeah. No, we don't suspect you of anything, just, we need to— Yeah. Thanks."

Shigata didn't say anything; he just sat and watched Quinn, who didn't even know what they were supposed to ask, fumbling for questions.

Bob Kerns was in his mid-fifties; he was a genial-looking man with a shock of prematurely white hair and pale blue eyes, and he readily answered what little Quinn knew to ask. No, he didn't know Andrea Collins, but that didn't mean he hadn't met her. After all, he was the only gun shop in town, and if she'd wanted to buy a gun she'd have had to come to him or go out of town. And she might not have bought a gun, of course; she might have thought about it and changed her mind, or she might just not have gotten to it yet.

There was something odd about his eyes, Shigata thought; they not only didn't match his friendly expression; they didn't have any expression to them at all.

But he knew where he'd seen Kerns before. And he knew Kerns didn't know he knew.

He'd spotted part of the answer as they drove up, in the

form of a POW license plate on Kerns's Ford. He was the right age for it to have been Korea.

They were standing up to leave when he asked, apparently casually, "By the way, Mr. Kerns, I notice your shop is named K&S. Who's the S?"

Kerns laughed easily. "Oh, I should have changed the name years ago. There's not an S anymore. I did have a silent partner when I first started out, but he was never really involved in the running of the business. He just provided me the money to get started, and I bought him out years ago."

"What was his name, Mr. Kerns?"

"Well, now, I don't see that—"

"What was his name, Mr. Kerns?"

"Why do you—?"

"What was his name, Mr. Kerns?"

Kerns is going to break easily, Shigata thought coldly. He should have been me last night. I cried; he'd have died. I'm sorry for the people who were with him, wherever he was a POW.

Kerns squirmed a little, shook his head, and then said reluctantly, "Henry Samford. But really, Mr. Shigata, he no longer has anything to do with—"

"And no keys to the building, I suppose."

"Well, I—"

"You call him Sam, don't you?"

"I—Well, he—"

Quite pleasantly, Shigata said, "Mr. Kerns, I'm placing you under arrest at this time. Normally I'd wait for a warrant, but I really can't run the risk of your communicating with your boss."

"Really, Mr. Shigata! I can't imagine what you mean—"

"I mean you took your mask off too soon."

"My—what?"

"You thought by the time the handcuffs were unlocked that I was so deeply in shock I wouldn't remember anything else I saw. You took your mask off too soon. You were wrong. But then I guess you were hot. It's hot work, isn't it, swinging a heavy whip? Even when you're taking turns with somebody else."

Kerns stared at him. All the color was slowly draining from his face.

"Samford," Quinn said. "Shigata, Samford, he's the guy I was telling you about a little while ago, he's the guy that runs the *Sentinel.*"

"I thought he might be. I think we're going to be able to prove that garbage in Andrea's storage room came off the *Sentinel* press. You one of the Sons of Liberty, Mr. Kerns?"

If possible, Kerns's face went even paler. "How do you know about that?"

"Let's say we're smart. What's going to happen to your federal firearms license when I call in the ATF and get them to search your shop and your home? Not every weapon you own is legal, is it?"

"You don't have any probable cause—"

"I think I will, before I'm through. Al, you want to loan me your handcuffs?"

"Gladly."

"You bet Samford had to get his name off the business records of the store," Quinn said. "The place wasn't going to get a federal firearms license until he did—have a look at this.''

It wasn't a long rap sheet, as rap sheets go. But it included an arrest and conviction for felony drunk driving and felony manslaughter. And someone had written in pencil, ''Reported kidnap of two-year-old daughter probably hincky but not enough for search warrant.''

And it included an arrest on Wednesday. Creating a public disturbance. Complainant, Andrea Collins.

He'd listed as his next of kin a wife, Melissa Samford. The address was 1201 Nottingham Drive.

''Let's go,'' Quinn said.

''Uh-uh,'' Shigata said. ''Let's go get a warrant. *Then* let's go. Mister Henry Samford alias Sam isn't going anywhere. He doesn't know we're on him. And I don't want to run any risk at all of his getting off. Thing is, Al, this wasn't a KKK—or Sons of Liberty—operation. It was entirely personal, and it's probably going to take a month to sort out all the whys and hows. But—what's cause and what's effect? Hate breeds hate. And how long has he been peddling hate?''

twenty-one

QUINN STOPPED THE CAR AT THE CURB AND both men swung the doors open. It was a big house. Quinn was right; Henry Samford wasn't hurting for money.

And it wasn't going to be the routine arrest they'd both hoped to be able to make it. Because Sam—that must be Sam—was standing in the driveway beside the open trunk of a silver-gray Mercedes. He saw them, and he turned; he turned with an automatic in his hand. An automatic with a homemade silencer, the kind made from a mail-order kit and a soft drink bottle.

He raised the pistol but he never got a chance to fire it, because the two guns spoke at once and he fell, he fell almost in slow motion, spinning to his left, his ankles tangling around each other, and he sprawled on his side with his eyes open and his coat pulled away from his chest, and the last three jets of blood from his heart spattered against the fender of the Mercedes.

"I almost couldn't fire," Quinn said. "He looked so

much like you I almost couldn't pull the trigger." He holstered his revolver and walked toward the body.

"Funny," said Shigata, who'd already holstered. "I didn't have any trouble at all pulling the trigger." He looked impassively down. "Half Japanese, I think. And good plastic surgery. He must have hated himself—"

"And everybody else," Quinn agreed. "Now let's see if we can find out what this was all about."

They walked toward the house. The front door opened. She came out so fast they almost didn't see her coming, her hair flying, her face distorted, and neither man had time to draw before she'd fired the first time, clutching the little .22 in both hands, her eyes squeezed tight as if to shut out the sight as well as the sound. "You won't get her!" she was screaming. "Not Gail, you won't get Gail, you won't! You killed Lucie, you killed that boy, but I won't let you have my baby!"

She fired again. The first bullet had missed entirely; with the second Shigata staggered slightly. It hit high on his left shoulder and startled him into motion; he ran forward, shouting, "No, Al, don't shoot!" and he caught her before she had time to fire a third time. "Look at me!" he shouted into her face. *"Look at me! Who am I?"*

She opened her eyes. They were lovely eyes, blue eyes, Gail's eyes. She looked at him. "You're not Sam," she said faintly. The gun fell from her limp fingers. "You're not Sam. Sam got away. And I—I shot you—and you're not Sam."

"Sam's dead."

"No. Sam'll never be dead. Not ever. Not ever. Sam kills people. Nobody kills Sam." There was a huge bruise, green and purple, on her chin. There was blood on her face. And blood on Shigata's hands, his hands that were around her shoulders.

"You've been beaten. He's been beating you." Shigata's voice shook with renewed horror. She was so thin, so fragile in appearance, it was as if someone had been torturing Gail.

"Yes." She twisted easily out of Shigata's grasp. Shrugged. "He always does."

"What do you mean, he always does?"

She turned away from him. A little woman. Tiny. Slim. With blood soaking through the white terrycloth beach coverup she'd put on, with bruises on her face, burns on her arms, blood on her wrists soaking a torn piece of rope showing that she'd somehow freed herself. "He always does. He likes to. Only this was worse. He wanted me to tell where Gail is. And I wouldn't."

"Where Gail—Do you know where Gail is?"

"Oh, yes, I know. But I won't tell." She turned to go back inside the house.

It was an unconscious gesture of dismissal. She's in shock, Shigata thought. "What's your name?" he asked quickly.

"Melissa."

"Melissa. Come here. Look. Sam is dead. Quinn and I killed him. He'll never hurt you again. He's dead."

She looked unbelievingly at the body. She looked back at Shigata. "You look so much like him."

"I'm not like him. Do you live here?"

"Yes. I'm his wife." Eyes glanced casually at the body. "I mean I was."

"Will you let my friend and me go look through the

house without getting a search warrant? We're both kind of police. You don't have to let us. But we need to."

She shrugged. "I don't care. Go ahead. I'm not going to live here anyway."

Quinn walked past them, into the house.

"Where are you going to live?"

"I don't know. But not here."

"Melissa. Please tell me where Gail is."

"I won't tell anybody. You look too much like Sam."

He took a deep breath. "Melissa. Touch my back. Under my shirt. Touch."

"Why?"

"Just do it. Then you'll see why."

He didn't let his face say that she was hurting him. But she knew; her face told him that his suffering went from her exploring fingertips into her own body, which already had enough to bear. She looked at his face, looked puzzled. "Sam did that? He hit you too?"

"Yes."

"I thought he just hit women. Why did he hit you?"

"Because I'm Mark Shigata. Does that name mean anything to you?"

He could tell it did. But her answer was altogether unexpected. "That was Sam's name," she said. "Before he changed it. Samford. That was his mother's name, before she got married. I wasn't supposed to know. Nobody was. But I found that paper. In the study. When he was in jail. I never told him I knew. But I always wondered, after I saw your picture."

"Wondered?"

"If that was why Wendy married you. Because you look

like Sam. She—liked Sam. But—I was married to him. Before she met him. You look like Sam."

"I'm not like Sam," he said. "I'm—I think—I think I must be his cousin. But I hadn't seen him in thirty years. I'm not like Sam." He'd think later, when he had time to think about it, that he'd killed his cousin. He'd come to terms with that later. But now he had other things . . .

Almost without his knowing it, his hand rose to her face, his thumb curled around the line of her cheek. She looked at him, her eyes wide. "I'm not like Sam," he repeated. "Please tell me where Gail is. Your baby, I know that, but my daughter now. Please tell me. I won't hurt you for not telling me. You know that. Nobody has any right to hurt you. But I need to know. For Gail's sake I need to know. She's my daughter and I love her. Please—"

Wide blue eyes widened further, as his hand moved tenderly around her face. She wasn't Gail. She was a woman, she was Melissa and although he'd never seen her before, they were bound together by love for Gail, and by something else, by something very strong, and he wanted her—he wanted her—he wanted her with a need he'd never felt for Wendy. With both of them hurt and cut and bruised, with the blood running down inside his coat from the bullet she'd put in his shoulder, with the body of the man she'd been married to crumpled on the grass eight feet away, he wanted her and he almost certainly would never have her, because he looked too much like Sam.

He wondered what she would look like not dazed, not in pain, not in shock.

He hoped it was his bullet that had killed Sam. Sam had her. And so he would never have her.

And the adoption hadn't been legal. He'd thought it

was, he'd acted in good faith, but he knew now that it wasn't.

She'd have Gail back. She'd have Gail back and he'd be altogether alone, just as he'd been all his life, only more alone now because now he would know he was alone.

But he stayed controlled; his hand caressing her face wasn't shaking, only he was saying, "Please—please—please—" and he didn't know whether he was asking Melissa for Gail or for Melissa. "Please—please—" and he'd be kissing her in a minute if he didn't watch out—"Please—" He'd been through too much, he couldn't stand any more, not any more at all—"please, please, please—"

And she kissed his caressing hand.

Kissed his hand and looked astonished, and he felt completely naked, and he was silent, quite still in the afternoon.

Quinn came out the front door. "Shigata."

The sound of his voice—Shigata's head jerked toward him, the spell utterly broken. "Al. What is it? What—"

Quinn was holding something dark blue. "It's Mark's jacket. My son's jacket. Mark's jacket. In the garage." His eyes were pools of grief and rage.

Melissa looked at it. "It's that boy's," she said. "I found it. Later. He'd taken it off in the kitchen when he was getting a drink of water. I was afraid to let Sam see it. So I hid it. In the garage. It's that boy's. Sam killed him, you know. He didn't tell me, but I know he did. Sam killed him."

"Why?" Quinn's voice was as slow as if the one word had been dragged out of him a letter at the time.

"Because he was going to call the police. I hired him

to dig a flower bed. But he dug up Lucie. I didn't remember that was where Lucia was buried."

"Lucie?" Shigata asked.

She told them about Lucie. She told them about the boy. She told them what Sam did to her then.

"How many years has that bastard been torturing you?" Quinn asked.

She looked at him, looked puzzled. Her voice was quite matter-of-fact as she answered. "Oh. Fifteen years, I guess. Darlene drowned. Lucie's mother. Darlene. She drowned. He wanted to marry me, you see, and he said it was very lucky Darlene fell in the swimming pool. He killed her, of course. But I didn't know that. Not until later. Not until too late. Then he told me. He told me he'd kill me if I ever tried to leave him. And he'd kill me if he ever got tired of me. I couldn't leave. Because of Gail. I had to have the money to give Wendy, for Gail, and there wasn't any other way I could get it. Sometimes I used to wish he'd get tired of me. It would be so nice to be dead. But I couldn't let him get tired of me. Because I was afraid if I was dead Wendy would give Gail back to him. My sisters were the only friends I had. And Wendy wasn't a very good friend."

Quinn turned to look at the body sprawled beside the silver car. "I'm glad Mark tried to call the police," he said, his voice shaking. "I'm glad of that. I'm glad he died for something. If he had to die."

"What happens to me now?" Melissa didn't sound as if she cared; she was asking out of curiosity only.

Quinn shook his head. "Why should anything happen to you? Hasn't enough already happened to you? Fifteen years of being that animal's punching bag, isn't that enough?''

"But—but I shot—''

"Clearly an accident,'' Shigata said firmly. "It was, you know. You meant to be shooting him. And there's not a jury in the world that could call you shooting him anything but self-defense.''

"Gail. What happens to Gail? Wendy's dead. Wendy can't keep her anymore. And I don't have any money. I can't take care of her.''

"You don't have to. Just tell me where she is. Tell me and I'll get her and take her home.''

"Yes. All right. I saw her. Last night. About an hour before Sam got me.'' She told them where she saw Gail.

Quinn raced for a phone, returning moments later to report, "Hoa. That's what he kept trying to call me about. He took her to Nguyen right after we left the house this morning. Nguyen has her now, has her in the kitchen making cookies for her daddy. She's safe, Mark, she's all right. And I've called an ambulance. I should have done that already. We don't need to be trying to search a house with you two standing there bleeding. That can wait. The house isn't going anywhere.''

Melissa looked at him. "The boy was yours?''

"Yes. The boy was mine.''

"He didn't look like you.''

"He looked like his mother.''

"I'm sorry,'' she said. "I'm really sorry. He was a nice boy.''

She could have called the police any time in fifteen years. But she didn't realize that; there is the psychology of the captive. Shigata knew about it, and he hoped Quinn did too.

Apparently Quinn did, because he answered, "Yes. He was a nice boy. And I know you're sorry." He turned. "Shigata."

"Yeah?"

"You've got a three-bedroom house. Can't you give this lady a place to stay at least for a few days, while she tries to pick up the pieces of her life?"

"I was going to," Shigata said with dignity, watching the ambulance turn the corner, wishing it would hurry, hoping there was some Demerol aboard.

"I was afraid you might not. And Shigata?"

"Yeah?"

"My department still needs a chief of police."

Very slowly, Mark Shigata smiled. "Yes. It does, doesn't it?"

afterword

SHIGATA'S SELF-DESPISING FAMILY IS IN fact not the portrait of any Nisei family I have ever known. The idea was the outgrowth of my relationship with an Anglo friend whose Mexican-American husband was utterly outraged to return from sea duty and find his wife industriously teaching Spanish to their five children so that they could communicate with their grandparents.

Shigata's aunt was suggested to me by my mother. A dear friend of hers, a Nisei woman, did indeed shoot herself on the day of the bombing of Pearl Harbor, and my mother was still mourning her death forty years later. She said to me, "I don't know why she did that. Nobody would have blamed her."

My mother was, of course, wrong.

ANNE WINGATE is a former police officer, serving on police forces in Georgia and Texas, where she was a qualified latent-fingerprint expert. Her tour of duty in Galveston provided the background for DEATH BY DECEPTION. She now lives in Utah.